SUNSPOTS

Gary Martin

Copyright © 2016 by Gary Martin

All rights reserved. No part of this publication may be reproduced, distributed, or transmitted without the express consent of the author.

Cover artwork and ship blueprints by Gary Martin

First edition

ISBN-13: 978-1519373311

for Cheryl

Acknowledgements

My thanks to Fraser, Polly, Claire, Nathan, Dave, Stella, Adam, Ben, Jon, Julie and Colin for letting me rope them in as test readers.
A special big thanks to Oli, who edited the hell out of it, and taught me a thing or two in the process.

MERCURY IV CLASS CARGO SHIP

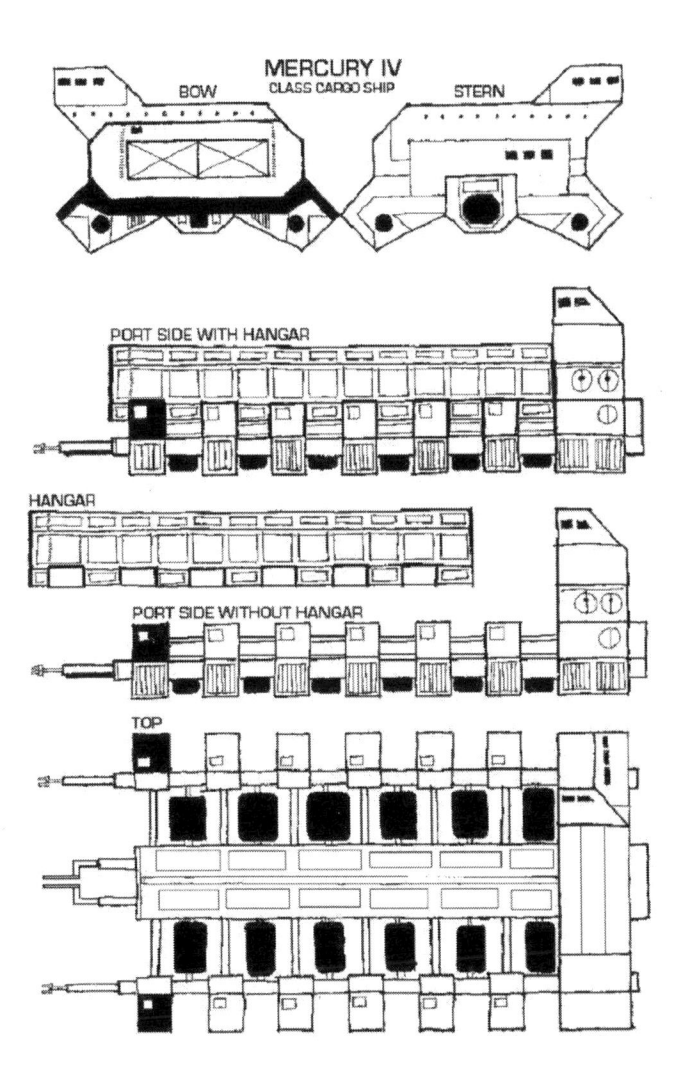

BOW

STERN

PORT SIDE WITH HANGAR

HANGAR

PORT SIDE WITHOUT HANGAR

TOP

1

I always thought that if you were in charge of a crew on a ship you were the Captain, it was as simple as that. My name is John Farrow and I'm in charge of a crew on a ship. Annoyingly for me, I'm not the Captain. I'm just a shift manager, and only in charge of half the crew. The other half I don't really see except for on changeovers, and then it's only for a few minutes.

This wasn't a job that I wanted, and I certainly didn't earn it by standing out or trying hard. I was working on the forklifts at the loading docks when it was offered to me. Nobody wanted it, and I wasn't given a choice.

I've now been in this position for three years, the

money's pretty good and I don't really do much except for the paperwork, assigning the odd duty, and reading a shit load of books. My crew pretty much manage themselves, which saves me a lot of time and hassle. I only really step in if there's an issue, or someone throws a tantrum. It rarely happens, but when it does it always seems to blow over quite quickly.

We work on a two crew system, and there are four people on each shift, with a payload specialist or *dump tech'* straddling both. The shifts are twelve hours, Monday to Sunday, for three solid months. It's a long slog, with no time off until we get back.

Our ship is called *Sunspot 2*. Her crew section has four decks. Deck one is the bridge and shift manager's (Captain's) office. Deck two is the habitation deck, with wash facilities and a small rarely used sickbay. Deck three is the recreation deck, the cargo bay and escape pods, and deck four is the engine room. There's a ladder that joins all four decks, it goes from the bridge straight down to the engine room, with hatches between each deck in case of decompression or fire. Each deck also has an escape airlock. The entire front three quarters of the ship is a massive hangar bay that's constantly filled to the brim with old storage containers, full of anything and everything horrible you can think of. Any redundant space on the outer hull is covered in a patchwork of solar panels, put there by hundreds of energy companies wanting to exploit our proximity to the sun. This probably makes the company more money than the waste disposal does.

There are two ships in the *Sunspots Waste Disposal* fleet, if you can call two ships a fleet. *Sunspot 1* works the three months we're back home and vice versa. Both ships are old *Mercury IV* class cargo haulers, about the size of small super tankers. They've been converted with heavy-duty heat shields so we don't burn to death when we reach our destination. We transport waste from all of Earth's colonies from a massive depot on the Moon, and take it to be incinerated in the Sun's corona. We're basically bin men.

This is my sixth three-month stint, and we're on day thirty-two. Everyone has settled in after his or her three months off, but no one is in the zone, and probably won't be for a while. At least the ship is working as well as it usually does, which is only just. Everything in the engine room clanks and grinds and buzzes at alarming levels. I'm not anywhere close to being mechanically minded, and have been told many times that everything is fine, but it really doesn't sound happy. Nothing gets replaced if it can be bodged back together, and everything has been bodged back together so many times I'm surprised anything works.

2

I'm sitting in the office behind the bridge waiting for Tom, the manager on the opposite shift to take over from me. I finished everything I had to do hours ago, and have been trying my best to look busy ever since. I've made sure everything is tidy and as close to the way he likes it as I can. I don't really fancy being the brunt of one of his reports again, but until I get any sort of official reprimand from up above, I'll continue to do just enough to get by. It'll do.

The door opens and Tom comes in yawning.

"Hey John, anything interesting to report?" he asks.

"No, nothing interesting at all," I reply and move from behind the desk.

"I hear that. Anything to actually report though?"

"Nope, just Robert bitching and moaning about everything."

"The usual then," he says and sits down in the chair I've just vacated.

"Afraid so. Don't think that'll change anytime soon. See you in twelve."

I walk out on to the bridge and see Kerry getting up from the pilot console. Her opposite slides in without a word. Mark is sitting at the navigation and communication station, and still waiting for his.

Kerry looks at me with glassy red eyes. The pink hair framing her face is beginning to look unkempt and slightly greasy after the twelve hours.

"Why do we have to have the night shift?" she asks.

"Good question," I reply, squinting through the small tinted viewports at the sun ahead of us.

"Well … the sun is always shining out here, and it's also constantly dark. I don't really think it makes a lot of difference either way."

She looks at me for a few seconds.

"A shit answer," she says.

"Thanks."

I move to the ladder and climb down to the habitation deck, and open the door to my quarters. It's a tiny room with a bed, a wardrobe, a toilet, a sink and just enough room to stand.

I sit on the bed and wonder if I should go to sleep now, and have a few hours free time before my next shift, or go to the rec deck now and have some food. That would mean listening to Robert or Mark go on and on about how awful they think the company is, or their take on the various wars happening on Earth or Mars, but at least it would be sociable. I stand up and leave my quarters. I'm hungry anyway, and there are far too many things to be thinking about by myself.

I climb down to the rec deck. The room's about ten metres by twenty, with two large tables set up in the middle, and a pool table where the third should be. There are some snack and drinks machines against the far wall and a large door into the storage area. There's an old holobox in the corner, which has relatively good signal until we get to about Venus, and then it quickly craps out. There are three large rectangular windows on the long wall facing aft. The main meal dispenser is next to the ladder I've just climbed down. The only people down here at the moment are Kerry and Tim. He's standing by the coffee machine, his uniform is immaculately ironed as usual, and his black hair is slicked back with some sort of product. He looks around as my feet hit the deck plates.

"Do you fancy a hot or cold beverage, John?" he asks in his odd accent.

"No thanks. I have my own card for that."

"Okay, maybe next time then," he says.

"Yeah, maybe I will."

He nods, and then walks past me without a drink of his own and climbs the ladder.

"I think he was waiting for you," Kerry says.

"Fucking dump techs. They're only ever with us for one trip, and without fail every single one of them tries too hard to fit in. It always makes me feel awkward," I say and look down at what she's eating. It's something brown from a plastic tray, and she's not looking entirely happy about it. She looks up.

"It's amazing to think they take a huge chunk of our wages for this fucking slop," she mutters.

I look closer at her tray, and then shake my head.

"Why do you always choose the worst thing on the menu then?"

"The picture looked good," she says and smiles.

"And it kind of reminds me of the sort of shit my first husband used to cook for me and the kids. When I was at back home long enough to eat with them at least, anyway. He was a fucking terrible cook."

"Your first husband?" I ask. I didn't realise she'd been married more than once.

"Yeah, he was the nicest person you'd have ever met. Probably would have got on well with you actually, John. He looked after our little girl and boy and kept the house up together while I was out piloting commercial jet liners on fucked up shift patterns," she says and continues eating.

"You have kids? So what happened? Did you guys split up?"

"No. One night, his brain just popped in his sleep."

"Oh shit, I'm really sorry," I say, feeling really

guilty that I'd asked.

"Don't be, it was about ten years ago. I miss him still, but it almost doesn't seem real anymore. Like a fucking idiot though, I married someone else about six months later, mainly to mask the pain I think. But he turned out to be a bastard, and my kids pretty much disowned me for it. My life sort of fell apart after that, and after more than a few bad decisions I ended up working here, possibly the worst paid pilot position in the whole solar system." She shrugs her shoulders and continues with her food.

"… I'm sorry … ," I say again, not knowing how else to respond.

"You really don't need to keep apologising," she says. "I love this job. It got my life back on track."

"Well, thanks for that. But why are you telling me?" I ask.

"It was his birthday yesterday, and I've been feeling a bit shitty because I forgot about it. This is between us, okay?"

"I didn't hear nothing."

"Anyway, weren't you supposed to be choosing something disgusting from the food dispenser?"

"I guess I was."

I look at the machine and the choices available. There are only seven, and to be fair, the carefully shot photos next to each selection do look quite appetising.

"The pictures don't quite do the meals justice do they?" I say.

"I've tried all seven, and this is the best one. And it's fucking horrible" She grimaces, but has now almost finished.

I insert my card and choose the chicken fricassee, it's one of two I haven't tried so far this trip. I've never had much of a problem with the microwave meals from this machine, and they change them every voyage to stop you going mad. I hear the whirring noise as it's being nuked, and a clunk as it drops into dispenser. I take it over to the table and tear off the plastic film and take a mouthful.

Fucking hell.

The chicken tastes like it's been soaking for days in bleach. If it wasn't for the fact that your card only lets you have three meals a day, I'd have spat it out, set fire to it, and ejected it from the airlock. I walk to the drinks machine and get a coffee, hoping that if I drink some of that rancid piss after every mouthful, it might wash away the taste of the fricassee. It does, to a degree.

"I think you've hit the fuckin' jack pot there," Kerry says with a smile.

I look at her and stick my tongue out.

Robert comes up the ladder from the engine room, only just squeezing through the hatch. His tattooed dome, face, blond beard and boiler suit are smeared in black marks. He walks over to the holobox and turns it on.

"What a bastard shift. Seriously, if I have to sort

out anymore of Sam's *repair jobs* I think I'll explode," he says to the room. I start to feel sorry for Sam, as she now has to spend the next twelve hours fixing whatever it is Robert has *sorted out*. I wish I had her on my shift. She's really friendly and actually knows what she's doing. And if I'm honest, there's something about the way she wears her boiler suit undone to her waist, with a tight vest top that's always smeared in oil marks that makes me smile guiltily. Robert often sports a similar look, but it's the opposite of sexy when he does it.

"If we'd had anyone like her working in the engine room of the QE7, my dad and I would have booted her out for being completely incompetent," he continues.

Kerry looks up at him and sighs.

"Yes, we're all very impressed that your dad is the head engineer on the QE7, but I can't help but notice that you're here, and not there anymore. Any reason for this?"

He looks at her for a few seconds.

"I wanted to make my own way, and not live in my dad's shadow," he says defensively.

"That's pretty good reason, but why the fuck did you end up here? I mean it's a pretty big drop. Luxury liner to a garbage ship?"

Robert is beginning to look a little red and flustered, luckily Kerry seems to notice this and pulls away. Robert has the habit of going into sulks for days if he doesn't get his own way.

"Sorry Robert, just busting your balls. It's been a long shift," she says.

"That's fine," he says flatly. He then looks up and starts to smile slightly as he hears footsteps coming down the ladder from the bridge. It's Mark. The one person on board he spends most of his time with on and off of shift. He now has an ally.

"That's the last time, I'm sick of it," Mark says as his feet hit the deck plates.

"I'm not doing the jobs of two people anymore, and then get forced to wait fifteen minutes to be relieved by Ian. He's always late, it's completely unprofessional." He's clearly annoyed, and his sharp features combined with his red cheeks seem to make his white hair look more like a wig than usual.

"You probably shouldn't have tried to be the hero and agreed to do communications as well as navigation in the first place," Robert says.

"You're right, but I never for one minute thought it would be permanent."

"Two jobs for the price of one, they'll never change that now. That's what you get for being a jobsworth. All the work and none of the glory."

"I'm not a jobsworth Bob, I just like to do things properly."

"You bloody well are. All that overtime you do on our time off? For standard pay as well," Robert says and shakes his head slightly.

"I get forced into it. I have no choice, I don't want to do it," Mark protests.

"No one is forced into overtime Mark. You can either say yes or no."

"Whatever," Mark says and then waves hand above his white hair and that's the end of that conversation.

"Is there anything interesting on the holobox?" he then asks.

"No, not for your depraved tastes anyway," Robert replies.

"I guess not. But then, I'm pretty sure my viewing tastes have been warped by the films you've let me borrow, Bob."

Kerry shakes her head.

"If this conversation ends up going where I think it might, you two can just fucking stop now," she says.

"Come on Kezza," Robert says smiling. "You absolutely love it! I bet you even starred in a few in your prime, what was that, about sixty years ago?" He looks over to Mark for a reaction.

She looks at him with daggers and raises an eyebrow.

"Fuck you, Robert," she says slowly and calmly, but Robert continues to plough on.

"I mean, you've been around a bit ain't ya? You've probably been in hundreds of 'em. Though at your age, it's probably been a while now since you've had a real man, eh, Mark, eh?"

He looks again to Mark for support, but Mark says

nothing, and just looks out of the viewports and then at the holobox.

"I think I've seen enough *real* men in my time, Robert, and none of them were that impressive," Kerry says, still calmly.

"You obviously haven't met an actual *real* man then, like me," Robert points at himself and smiles.

"Now I am impressive, I'm a young virile male, with an above average sized appendage," he says, now pointing down at his crotch.

She looks at him and sighs.

"It may well be above average, but I doubt anyone could find it under all that disgusting blubber. I mean for fucks sake, have you ever actually looked at yourself?"

Robert stares at her, and looks genuinely shocked.

"No need to get so personal, I was only joking around with you," Robert says indignantly.

"Too bad you're not funny then," Kerry says.

Robert looks to Mark once again for support. When none comes he looks at me.

"John, you can't let her talk to me like that."

"I'm sorry, I'm off duty. And to be fair, you did start it," I reply.

"I didn't, Kerry started it when she said I was kicked off of the QE7," he shouts. There are a few seconds of silence, and I look at him.

"She didn't say that, Robert," I say. He looks around the table, I'm feeling a little bit uncomfortable.

"You can all go fuck yourselves," he snarls, then pulls a face that I guess is outrage and stomps to the vending machine, chooses something, grabs it and awkwardly climbs up the ladder to his quarters.

When we hear the door slam, everyone bursts out laughing.

"What a prick," Mark says while wiping his eyes.

"I think that's enough entertainment for me for one morning, time for bed," I say and stand up.

"You do realise he probably won't talk to anyone now," Mark says.

"And you think that's a bad thing?" I say. "Anyway, I thought you guys were quite close."

"Yeah, but he's way too much work sometimes," Mark replies.

"All the time," Kerry says.

"True. See you guys later. Nighty night," I say and climb the ladder to my quarters.

3

I splash my face with water and look at myself in the mirror. I'm getting old. The receding hairline isn't too obvious yet, but there are a lot of greys going on. Not too many lines on my face, but I've constantly got bags under my eyes.

I'm not usually one to dwell on things like age, but I'm beginning to feel like life might actually be passing me by. I'm nearly forty, I'm not married and don't have any children. That was a conscious decision, I really didn't want kids. Right up until recently, it seemed like a terrible idea, settling down and having a family. All the normal things all the normal people do. I've never felt grown up enough for it.

It's beginning to occur to me that maybe no one's

grown up enough for it. The conversations about having children always ended the same way, with me not backing down. And the way I left everything back home before I got the shuttle here, oh dear. I may have fucked everything. And now I'm basically hiding for three months.

I lay down on the bed and all I can see is Ez's face. The way she looked the last time I saw her. And now I've completely abandoned her.

I honestly start thinking that there's no point trying to go to sleep, as my mind won't shut up, but I'm asleep in minutes.

I get woken up suddenly by a high-pitched squeal, followed by a low rumbling noise. It goes on for a time and then stops. After a few minutes of listening to silence, I'm not really sure if I've heard anything at all. I look at the alarm clock in my half asleep daze and it's something past eleven in the morning. My alarm is set for three, so I close my eyes and go back to sleep. What only seems like seconds later I hear the beeping of the alarm, and bang my hand on the snooze button. I need to snooze it at least four times before allowing it to rip me out of sleep fully.

I get out of the covers and sit on the edge of the bed, staring at the wall for a few minutes. I then stand up and take a piss, flush the toilet, grab a towel then leave my quarters and head for the washroom. I stop halfway down the corridor and realise everything seems a little too quiet. The dull hum of the engine room seems to have stopped. Without thinking, I knock on Kerry's door, to see if she knows anything about this.

She opens her door looking more tired than I do.

"What do you want?" she says, then looks down then up again and smiles. "Are you propositioning me?"

I look down and realise I'm still only in my pants.

"Oh fuck," I say and quickly wrap the towel around me. Flustered, I ask if she has any idea why the engines have stopped.

"It's your job to know that shit isn't it?" she replies bluntly.

"I guess so, but I've only just woken up."

"So have I, you daft twat. Why would I know more about it than you?" she says and rolls her eyes.

"Fair point, I'll get changed and ask Tom. Maybe a bit later, after I've showered."

"Piss off and let me sleep then," she says and slams the door in my face.

I continue to the washroom, open the hatch, walk past the two curtained off baths and to the farthest shower cubicle. I turn the tap on and move back as fast as I can so I don't get hit by the freezing water. I then stretch my arm around the flow and turn the dial, hopefully I can get it somewhere between hot and cold, and not the usual hot then cold then hot then swearing that usually happens with these things. I put my hand in, and I seem to have hit the sweet spot. I stand in the shower and close my eyes. Ez pops into my head again, and I wash myself and try and think of anything else unsuccessfully. I dry off and walk back to my quarters, brush my teeth and get into my uniform. I should probably go and see Tom, and find out what's going on, and see if it has anything to do with the noise I possibly heard in my sleep this morning.

I leave my quarters and climb the ladder to the bridge, and bang my head on the hatch.

"Fuck it," I shout. The hatch is never closed. I turn the wheel and press the two switches and it opens onto the bridge. I pull the top section of ladder down so I can climb up and then walk to the shift manager's office. You can still see the indentation of the word *Captain* underneath the cheap sticker that says *Shift Manager's office*. I've always wanted to change it back and see if anyone noticed. I knock three times and go in.

I look at the desk and Tom's not there. I guess if there are engine troubles, he's probably going to be with Sam in the engine room helping her to sort it out. I walk back out onto the bridge to see if Will or Ian have any idea what's happening, but their seats are empty as well. Confused, I walk to the Pilot's console, and look to see if there's anything I can figure out by looking at the screens. It may as well be in Japanese, I have no fucking idea what any of it means. I really should have paid some attention when Kerry showed me some of the basics, as I'm supposed to be able to cover the position if something were to happen.

Will and Ian must be with Tom and Sam in the engine room, if they're all down there, something serious must have happened. I stare out of the view ports for a second. Then it hits me. For fucks sake, they're in the canteen having their last break before we take over.

My shift doesn't tend to take breaks together, but Tom's shift has been known to. I feel pretty stupid, but it's probably best to think the worst out here. I get on the ladder and climb down to the habitation deck, and notice the hatch between habitation and the rec deck is closed too. I'm surprised I didn't notice that when I went from here up to the bridge. Tired I guess. I open the hatch and climb down.

"You bunch of bastards," I shout over my shoulder as I clear the hatch. I jump three rungs from the bottom and turn around. The rec deck is completely empty.

A cold chill goes down my spine, I guess they are all in the engine room after all. A question then pops into to my mind, now I'm down here, should I have breakfast? Or check the engine room and make sure everything is alright and then have it? I suddenly realise how inappropriate that is, and quickly push it from my mind.

Once again, oddly, the hatch is closed. I open it and climb down to the lowest deck. The air down here always has a metallic aroma, kind of burning metal, with a strong oil smell just underneath it. Everything smells almost normal now, just a faint hint. The room is pretty big, with a huge covered shaft that runs from one end to the other, with the solar energy storage and main generators on the far side. The shaft is completely covered in tubes and wires and control panels and lots of other things that I have no idea about. There's a gangway that runs above it and either side of it. At the end of each gangway is a small hatch, which gives you access to the inspection tubes that run underneath the hangar deck and above the fuel tanks that run the entire underside of the ship. The tubes are no more than a metre and a half in diameter, and you have to be on your hands and knees to get through them. Robert isn't a fan as he can hardly fit, and I'm not a fan because like any normal person, small spaces freak me out.

It's really quite eerie down here with the engines not running. Normally it sounds terrifying, as if the engine is on the verge of tearing itself apart. But now, nothing. Just dead silence. I shout out Tom's name, the echo bounces around a few times, but I don't get an answer. There are plenty of places to hide down here, and usually you'd have to hunt for someone if they weren't at their station because of the deafening racket. But now, in this silence, if anyone were down here, they would have heard me.

I begin to feel nauseous. The fear is slowly building

up in my body. There is no way that they're all in the inspection tubes, absolutely no way. But I have to look.

The small ladder to the first gangway takes me seconds to clear. I then stand staring at the first hatch. I don't want to open it, I'm afraid of what happens if they're not in there. What the fuck do I do then?

The wheel turns easily, and I press the two switches. The hatch opens with a hiss. I peer in, it's dark, but I can pretty much see all the way to the front of the ship. Empty.

With a small push, the hatch closes and I climb the metal steps to the gangway above the shaft. I open it. That tube is empty as well.

Heavy footed, I walk down the steps to the last gangway. I almost don't bother to open the hatch, it makes no sense that they'd be in there. Not all of them anyway. I finally open it and it's the same as the rest. Empty.

One half of this crew has completely vanished. I can't quite get this idea into my head, it doesn't make sense. There's nowhere for them to go. I can feel my throat getting tight, and I loosen my top button, I can taste bile building up and before I know it, I vomit over the engine shaft. I take a deep breath and realise that I haven't stopped being sick yet, and start choking on it. I try to breathe in but can't, I try again and it's like trying to breathe through polythene.

Fully panicking now, I throw myself at the wall

above the hatch, back first, hoping that I may dislodge some of the sick. I still can't breathe, I throw myself again, and still nothing. My vision starts to cloud and I try one more time, as hard as I can before I've lost all of my strength.

Hitting the wall at the wrong angle, I lose balance and topple over the safety rail. I fall about five feet and land full force on my back. I'm in agony, but seem to be able to breathe again. Not very well, it hurts as I try, but air is now getting through.

I lay there for what seems like ages, I try to process what's happening, but at the moment I'm completely at a loss. I wait until I'm breathing without effort and then try to get up. Oh fuck that hurts. I use the safety rail to help me, and then use it to steady myself. I climb the ladder back on to the gangway then the stairs and get back to the other side. Once down, I walk over to a control panel and press the big red emergency button. The alarm goes off, loud enough to wake up the dead.

4

I'm sitting alone on the middle table of the rec deck, I've been here for more than five minutes and still no one has arrived. The alarm is ringing out loudly and I can barely hear myself think. I'm scared. I don't want to be the only person on board. I'm assuming everyone on my shift knows that the rec deck is the emergency meeting area. The cargo bay beyond the drink and snack machines has the only two escape pods in it, so it's the only place on board that would really make any sense. But I'm still here alone. Just as I'm about to properly go into a full panic mode, I hear clanking on the ladder. I sit up straight, and try to look like I know what's happening.

I'm relieved that Mark arrives first, and at the moment he's still wearing the long johns he slept in, and looks barely awake. He sits at the table opposite me and asks what's going on. I look up and tell him to wait until everyone else arrives. Kerry's next, looking a lot more awake than she did earlier and already in her uniform, or costume as she calls it. Tim climbs down next, looking as well presented as ever. He offers everyone a drink, but no one takes him up on his offer.

We then sit for what seems like an age for Robert to arrive. I start hoping that maybe he's disappeared as well, when we all finally spot his fat arse climbing through the hatch from the habitation deck. He sits down, and doesn't say anything, which is unusual for him. I'm guessing he's still sulking. I walk to the control panel on the wall and turn off the alarm.

"Okay," I say. "We have a massive problem."

Mark looks and me.

"Aren't we going to wait for the rest of the crew to arrive? Be rude to start without them," he says.

"That's the problem," I say. "They're gone."

Everyone around the table stares at me.

"What the fuck do you mean they're gone?" Kerry asks.

"They're just gone. I noticed that the engines had stopped when I got up, and when I went to see Tom about it, he wasn't in our office," I say.

Robert looks at me like I need to be stepped on.

"You set off the emergency alarm because Tom wasn't in his office? You complete fucking prick, I knew you were a useless cunt but this is … "

"Fuck you Robert. There was no one on the bridge

either, or the rec deck, or the engine room, or in the inspection tubes. They have vanished into thin fucking air."

"Shut up, the pair of you," Kerry shouts. "John, what's happened to them then? They can't have just disappeared. It's not possible. There's really nowhere to go."

Mark shakes his head and looks completely confused.

"I don't understand, how can they just be gone? We've got to tell the company," he says.

"Not until we have something to tell them. I have no idea where they've gone, but we'll have to find out, and pretty soon," I say.

Robert looks up from the table with a smile on his face.

"You've checked everywhere, yes?" he says slowly.

"Yes," I reply, even slower.

"When you say everywhere, you mean everywhere right? Even say, the hangar?" he says and leans back in his chair.

I stare at him. My heart stops. The thought hadn't even occurred to me to check it. The hangar is by far the biggest part of the ship, about four times the size of the entire crew area, and I hadn't even considered looking there. What do I say to this without looking like a complete idiot? I have no idea. I'm stumped, and I know there's really no point lying about it.

"Um … no," I manage, and look down at the table.

There is a dead silence, and I can feel the smugness burning off of Robert like a fire.

"Well there you have it ladies and gentlemen, our manager is officially a useless piece of shit," he says, grinning and clearly no longer sulking.

Mark then starts laughing.

"I can't believe you didn't check the hangar, of all the places not to check. It's massive! But I guess it's so chocked full of waste containers it would have taken hours. Lazy fucker!" he says.

Great, they're a tag team again. Lucky me.

Kerry gives Mark a sharp look, his face drops and he looks away. She looks straight at Robert.

"Why would Tom, Sam, Will and Ian be in the hangar? I mean one or two of them, yeah, it's fuckin' possible, but all four of them? That doesn't make any sense. None at all. Did you think about that before you decided to rub John's nose in it? I don't fucking think so," she says loudly.

He looks at her and lowers his head slightly, looking a little deflated, and says nothing.

"I suppose I better check it then." I say quietly.

I get up, and walk to the door between the snack and drink machines. The cargo bay has the only entry into the hangar on the whole ship, and it occurs to me that I haven't checked in here either. I open the door and look around, the two escape pods are in place, and there are a few boxes piled up here and there, but nowhere really to hide.

"Tom," I quietly shout. No answer. He's not here, and I almost feel glad about it. I turn right toward the hangar's airlock and punch in the code to open the door. It beeps angrily at me and lets me know in no uncertain terms that it's not going to open. That's a bit odd, so I type in the pass code again, but a lot slower to make sure I didn't get it wrong the first time. It beeps angrily again. I look through the small round window into the airlock, and then look at the far door. It's not there.

The sun is shining through the space where the door to the hangar used to be.

My heart stops again as I realise. Oh my fucking god, the entire hangar bay is gone.

I walk back to the rec area and stand in the door. Everyone stares at me.

"That was quick, I bet you've forgotten the code you complete cock," Robert says and looks around the table smiling.

I look at him.

"Have a look yourself, you fat fuck," I say.

In my head that was loud and aggressive. But I think I probably just mumbled it quietly. I seriously doubt Robert even heard it.

He gets up and barges past me to the hangar airlock. Kerry gets up and walks toward me.

"John, you okay? You look a little pale," she says, looking concerned.

"Where's the fucking hangar gone?" Robert shouts.

At that point, everyone decides to barge past me and have a look.

There's a lot of shouting and swearing going on in the cargo bay. I'm not sure what to do with myself, so I go and grab myself a coffee and sit back down at the table and nervously wait for them to return.

I've just about composed myself, when Kerry, Robert, Mark and Tim come single file through the door, and one by one sit down. I look around the table and try to put on an air of authority.

"As far as I can tell," I say "we're dead in the water. I don't know if the engines are working, or if we've had a major mechanical failure. So Robert, can you please get down there and see if you can figure out what's wrong, if anything?"

Robert stands up and looks at Mark.

"Are we actually going to listen to him? After what's just happened?" he says and then looks around the table. I take a sip from my coffee, which oddly tastes quite nice now and I'm about to reply, when after pretty much saying nothing for the whole trip, Tim finally pipes up.

"What exactly did he do wrong Robert? Tell me," he says.

Robert doesn't say anything, he just stares at Tim with a look of puzzlement on his face, for what seems like ages. I guess he thought everyone was firmly on his side. He then finally speaks.

"He called a meeting before he had all the

facts," he finally manages. "And he didn't check the hangar bay."

"Is that it? Is that all? So he forgot to check the hangar bay. But wait, it's not there anymore. Had he checked it first, we'd still be in exactly the same position. That hardly makes him a *"useless piece of shit"* as you called him. He pretty much had all the main facts. You petty, petty man."

I have to stifle a grin. I enjoyed that quite a lot. Maybe I will accept a drink from him the next time he offers.

"Robert, if you would, please can you check the engines," I say.

He says nothing, then stands up and walks to the ladder with his head slightly slumped, and climbs down to the engine room.

"Kerry, Mark, can you guys head to the bridge and see if you can find out where the hanger is now?" I ask, and then look at Tim.

"Tim, can you stay in the cargo bay and see if you can work out why the hangar went walkies? And um, thanks for that."

"Anytime John. I'm happy to help out any way I can," he says in his odd voice, and then walks to the cargo bay. I follow Kerry and Mark up to the bridge.

5

Mark sits at his station, puts on his headphones and mic, and looks at the screen. He pulls a face and beckons me over.

"Ian didn't log out, if you're going leave your station, even for a piss, you always log out," he says.

I look over to Kerry.

"Anything?" I ask.

"Same here at the pilot console, John," she says and shrugs her shoulders.

"Why wouldn't they have logged out? Something must have happened really quickly. Mark, can you scan for the hangar?" I ask.

"Already doing it, and as far as I can tell, it's about sixty kilometres ahead, and moving away from us toward the sun."

I look out of the tinted viewports, squint my eyes and can just make out a small rectangle silhouetted against the sun. I turn away, even with the specialised glass it's still pretty fucking bright.

"That's not too far away, but if Robert can't get the engines running, it may as well be on Pluto. My guess, is that Tom and his shift are on board, and after the engines failed, decided to continue the job using the hangar only. It has thrusters either side, top and bottom, so the dump tech' can aim it, I expect they also can be used to propel it. They'll just get to the usual safe distance, open the massive door on the front, use the pneumatic ram to expel all the waste containers into the sun, turn round and rendezvous with us. We all live happily ever after."

I think about what I've just said, it sort of explains what could have happened, but it just makes me realise how many unanswered questions there really are. Too many. I'm pinning all my hopes on the fact that Tom's shift are all over there, safe and sound, just doing their jobs, a tiny bit heroically. I didn't know that the hangar could detach, and neither did Robert. It's possible that Sam, The engineer who works opposite Robert knew this. She's young and enthusiastic enough to own all the manuals and blueprints. But to the best of my knowledge, since *Sunspots Waste Disposal Inc.* acquired the two ships around twenty years ago, they have never been separated. That would make doing it off the cuff really quite dangerous, for both parts of the ship. If our engines had failed, we'd radio for assistance, not take a joy ride. I also really can't believe all this would have gone down, and no one thought to tell us. No way.

"Mark, can you see if you can contact them?" I ask.

"Erm … I don't know if it can receive wireless transmissions when it's detached. If anyone's down there doing anything, we normally just talk through the intercom. You know, internally," he replies.

"I understand the concept of the intercom, Mark. Shit. Try as many frequencies as possible then, it may have some sort of old radio installed that hasn't been used for a while. Tom's crew are probably working on it now."

"Tom's a clever guy John, he knows our frequency, it might make sense to wait for them to contact us."

"Okay, see if you can contact the company then, and see what they think we should do," I say.

"Fine, but we've passed Venus, so it'll be a while before we get any response," Mark says.

"I know, and hopefully it'll all have blown over by then, but just in case, they can at least send a ship to tow us back. After that, can you contact Robert and see how he's doing down there?"

The last thing I wanted to do was go down to engineering and see if there was anything I could do to help, but I was running quickly out of ideas on the bridge.

"Actually, I'll go down and see if he needs an extra pair of hands," I eventually say.

Kerry gets out of her chair.

"I'll go with you, it may help to keep the pair of

you daft bastards civil," she says as she's walking towards the hatch.

"I can't really argue with that, in which case, I'll let you go first. He's probably in a sulk with everyone now," I say.

"Not me," Mark says with a grin.

Kerry flips him the finger and gives me a look that suggests I should man the fuck up, and then goes on ahead anyway.

We climb down the four levels and see Robert lying down underneath the main part of the engine shaft, with tools and parts all over the deck. How he managed to get under there god only knows. He sees us and awkwardly pulls himself out. He looks straight at Kerry, ignoring me completely.

"I tried to start the engines, but at the moment, they're dead. I've tried all the usual ways, and a few alternative start up procedures and still nothing. Normally this would mean one of a few things has happened. I've checked all the relays, the solenoids are working fine and the cooler system doors are opening and closing without resistance. I haven't checked the fuel tanks yet, it could well be a problem with the line somewhere," he tells her.

"You mean someone has to go into the inspection tubes?" I ask apprehensively.

He looks at me for a brief second then looks back at Kerry.

"The only place it can really go wrong is in the fuel

filters, or the line just before them. It's a very bad design. And it's about seventy metres on your hands and knees all the way to the front of the ship to get to them."

I get a horrible feeling I'm going to be asked to go in and have a look. Not that I'll know what I'm looking for. But instead, he asks Kerry.

"Kerry, you know the retro thruster junction box at the end? Big square thing, you'll have to take that off, and then you'll be at the filters. Just check for any obvious signs of blockage."

There is a silence as Kerry stares back at Robert, not looking happy. To be fair neither of them do.

"Robert, you're not my boss, and you don't give me orders. You can go fuck yourself if you think I'm going in the tubes again after last time." She says.

He looks at me and smiles.

"Oh yeah, last time she went in, I locked the hatches. Forgot she was in there."

And just like that, he's talking to me again. I clearly have no idea how his mind works or how to deal with him.

"Are you going in then?" I ask Robert sheepishly.

"That would be a big hairy no I'm afraid. I'm too big to do anything comfortably down there. I can get in, but I can't turn around. That scares the living shit out of me," he says, shaking his head.

"Oh great … I guess it's down to me then," I sigh.

Fucking hell fucking hell fucking hell. I can feel my

heart speeding up.

Robert grabs a couple of spanners from the tool rack and passes them to me.

"I'm not sure what size the bolts are on the junction box, but these should cover all the bases. Try not to electrocute yourself when you're taking it off."

"Electrocute myself? Is that likely?"

"Only if you're not careful, just move it slowly," he says.

"Can you not just turn off the power?" I ask.

"I can, but it means all the lights in the tubes will go out too. You don't want to be crawling down there with just a torch."

"No, I absolutely don't wanna do that."

I know what happens if you go into claustrophobic dark places with just a torch. It stops working. You hit it a few times, it works for a little while longer, and then it stops working for good. You then light a match, and that goes out as well. You start to light another one, but you hear a noise, you turn around, and then get eaten by monsters.

I put the spanners in my back pocket and climb the small ladder on to the first level of the gangway. I look back.

"Which tube?"
"Top one."

6

Walking up to the metal steps, I feel the same apprehension I had earlier. I stare at the hatch, I didn't want to open it then, and I really don't want to open it now. Lots of half formed excuses start coming into my head. I really hate tight spaces, and the panic is beginning to rise. Working on a spaceship was a very bad idea, and it wasn't even mine. I'm a fucking idiot.

I try my best to focus on the task at hand. I really have to force myself to open the hatch. I turn the wheel, then hesitantly press the two switches either side of it, and the hatch opens with a familiar hiss.

"About fucking time!" Kerry shouts.

"Screw you." I say back, slightly more aggressively than I mean it.

With one hand on the rung above it, I lower myself into the hatch. Now on my hands and knees, I crawl into the tube. I look back.

"Don't shut the hatch while I'm in here."

I start to move forward, the walls are a horrible shade of rusty brown, getting darker and more corroded at every seam, and I begin to notice how strong it smells in here. Like stale fuel. I start worrying that maybe we have a leak. I turn my head.

"It's possible we may have a leak, it smells of fuel in here, pretty badly," I shout behind me.

"It always smells like that, the tubes are attached to the fuel tanks, what d'you think it'd smell like in there?" Robert shouts back, with slight reverb on his voice. I'm not feeling reassured.

Crawling forward on my hands and knees, I look into every inspection hatch as I pass. Each one is full of tubes, wires and dials that mean nothing to me. They all look like they used to have covers, as I can see the screw holes at every corner, but they've all been lost over time, or more likely permanently removed. It would have been a nightmare constantly unscrewing the covers every time you wanted to look, then screwing them back on again in such a confined space. They probably didn't last more than two or three inspections before they were discarded. I try to keep my mind occupied with as many other thoughts as I can, hoping it'll stop me thinking about where I am.

I pass two smaller tubes joining this one either side of me, they're quite narrow, but have handholds. They both lead downwards at forty five degree angles into darkness. I'm assuming they go to the other two inspection tubes below me. Around about every four metres there's a small light on the ceiling of the tube, which leaves nice pools of darkness for me to crawl through, hiding away anything my imagination decides could be lurking there. I'm trying my best not to think of anything at all, but I'm completely failing. What could realistically be in here with me anyway? In all our years of space travel, the human race has never found anything resembling aliens, intelligent life, or monsters. The only things that could actually be in here with me are rats, but that's scary enough. I can't stand the hairy bastards.

As I crawl into another pool of darkness, my right hand slips on something and I fall on my face.

"Fuck it," I shout. It's too dark to see what I've slipped on, but it feels slimy, maybe oil. I wipe my hand on my thigh to get it off in case it's corrosive, and start crawling again.

I really wish I did have a torch now. Just keeping myself moving forward is becoming an issue, but I must be somewhere close to the halfway point. Suddenly, a loud metallic banging noise starts, it goes on for about two seconds then it stops. My eyes widen and my body tenses up, I stop dead. I wait a few seconds, but all I can hear is my breathing, almost to the point of hyperventilating. I wait for a minute or so, but hear nothing else. My breathing is almost normal again now, so I decide to continue.

I start to move forward, and suddenly it happens again. This time louder and continuously. I can't tell where it's coming from, as the sound is echoing and bouncing all around me. I don't think I'm going to be able to cope with this much longer, my heart is banging like a drum roll. I'm sweating profusely and I don't think my mind can keep it together. I close my eyes, then I curl up into a ball, put my hands on my ears and I scream. I keep screaming until finally the banging stops and everything goes silent.

I hear laughing echoing in from the direction of the engine room. Just one voice, and I know whose voice it is.

At this very moment, I want him dead, and I want it to be a horrible and painful death. The fat cunt.

I resolve to get to the junction box as fast as I can, open it up, check the filters, then head back to the engine room at my fastest possible crawling speed to smash that bastards head in with some sort of blunt instrument. I'll give him this, I'm not scared anymore. Though I doubt that was the point.

After a continued fast crawl, which is a lot harder to do than I would have thought, I finally get to the end and see the retro thruster junction box. It doesn't look like it belongs there, and reeks of a quick bodge job. I look around it, and on the underside and there are four bolts holding it in place. Three look about the same size while the other is considerably smaller. I'm going to have to get my hand in underneath it at an almost impossibly awkward angle, the bolts are bound to be a pain in the arse to undo, and there's the danger of dropping the spanner down the gap between the shaft and the fuel tank. In my current mind frame, I'm going to want to get it done as fast as possible. I'll probably end up doing something stupid, then hitting the junction box in frustration and then getting myself electrocuted.

I slide the thirteen-mil spanner out of my pocket, the three bigger bolts look roughly that size. I put my hand under the junction box to undo the first bolt, and have to twist my wrist to the point I can barely hold on to the spanner. I feel it lock into place around the bolt head, and I just have to hope the bolt's not on too tight. I then hear a loud buzz, and I instinctively let go of the spanner out of fear of being electrocuted. I hear it clatter on something, and with a dull thud it wedges in against a few rubber tubes and the tank. There's no way I can get to it now, it's lost. Bollocks. I pull my hand out and my wrist is already hurting from the angle it was at. I hear the buzz again, this time it's followed by a familiar noise. The lights dim slightly and the entire tube starts to gently vibrate. The engines have started up again. Fucking hell, Robert has actually figured out what was wrong.

It still takes a while, but I manage to crawl back to the engine room at a faster pace than I crawled in. When I get to the hatch I can see Robert is staring at a monitor, looking confused. I climb out and walk down the metal stairs and slide down the ladder. I walk up to him, fully ready to give him a mouthful for being a complete arsehole. But when he looks at me, I can see in his eyes that something is very, very wrong.

7

"It was sabotage," he says.

Slightly lost for words, I manage, "What?"

"It was sabotage, the engines were sabotaged. It was very, very subtle. It's impossible it could be anything else. It was enough to stop the ship dead without breaking it, but really easy to fix when it needed to be."

He holds up a spoon shaped piece of metal.

"They knew exactly what they were doing. If you put this between the drive manifold and the cooling chamber, the engines just stop."

He demonstrates by placing the piece of metal where he said. The engine stops with a slow decreasing whine.

"Fits perfectly too, I would have missed it if Kerry

hadn't suggested looking there."

He pulls it out and the engines screech back to life again.

We look at each other as we realise the implications. We're so screwed.

"Why would anyone want to sabotage a waste disposal ship?" I say, thinking out loud, but Robert answers anyway.

"Maybe they wanted the hangar, maybe it had something of value in it, and they wanted to disable us to get away with it?"

Not a bad idea, but it had one big thing going against it.

"Last I saw, it was heading directly towards the sun. That's not exactly a place to hide out with treasure. And who's *they* anyway?" I ask.

"I don't know, maybe a trained squad of elite assassins, sent here from a secret lair on … Uranus?" He smiles.

I just look at him.

"I'm going back to the bridge, I trust you can handle things down here?"

He holds up the piece of metal, and pulls a face.

"If I don't accidentally drop this back in place, I would have thought so."

With that I climb the ladder to the bridge as fast as I can. Halfway up I'm breathing heavily and I realise I haven't given him any sort of verbal abuse for what he pulled on me in the tube. It'll have to wait, as our situation has probably just got worse.

I'm fully out of breath by the time I get to the bridge, it's only a four deck climb, but I don't usually climb them all at once at that speed.

Kerry and Mark turn around in their seats and look at me. Mark is still in his long johns and his ruffled white hair is looking more like a wig than ever. I assume they're waiting for instructions. I wave them off while I get my breath back. They look at each other then back at me.

"Okay, okay, I need to do a bit more exercise and I need to eat less pizza."

"I didn't say a fuckin' word, but a definite yes to all of the above," Kerry says looking, slightly pleased with herself. Mark just grins.

"While you were helping Robert with the engines, I took the liberty of plotting an intercept course with the hangar," Mark says.

"Good work, have you sent Kerry the co-ordinates?"

"I got 'em, just give me the fuckin' order and we'll be underway, Captain," she says in an old movie pirate voice.

I have to admit, I really like the sound of that.

"The order is yours, Madame." I reply in a stupid voice of my own.

Kerry turns back around and presses a few buttons, flicks a few switches and moves the huge lever which controls acceleration forward on her console. The engines get audibly louder the further along the line she pushes it. It gets to the furthest point and she locks it off.

"Full steam ahead," she says and turns back around.

"Thank you," I say, and then look at Mark. "Realistically, how long at full speed will it take to catch up?"

He types something into his console that I can't see, then turns around.

"Judging on its speed, and our top speed about six hours I'd think, maybe slightly longer."

Kerry stands up and stretches, then leans on the edge of her console.

"The difficulty that we're going to face when we get there, is that none of us has ever coupled or uncoupled the two parts of this ship before. I think I can probably guide us into a decent position, coming at it from underneath, but fuck knows what we do from there," she says.

She's got a point. We all only found out it could do that when it decided to take a walk to the sun by itself, while we were all asleep. Just as I think we're getting somewhere, and things are actually beginning to look up, another problem rudely presents itself. An idea then pops into my brain.

"I'll be back in a second," I say and walk to my office. Once in, I open the grey cabinet and start looking through all the paperwork messily piled up at the bottom. Finally I see what I'm looking for and pull it out slowly while trying not to knock the precarious pile over in the process. It's a massive book, about thirty centimetres by forty, and about ten deep, dog eared and old. I hold it up to my mouth and blow on it, and am pretty disappointed to find there's not really any dust on it to blow away. I walk back out to Kerry and Mark and bang it on the console table.

"What is it?" Mark asks.

I look from Mark to Kerry with a big grin on my face and clap my hands once.

"This, my good man, is how we're going to solve our coupling problem," I say. They both look at me blankly.

"It's only the bloody instruction manual!"

Kerry rolls her eyes.

"You absolute fucking idiot. I actually thought you may have a decent solution up your sleeve. Bloody instruction manual, you prick," she says and shakes her head.

"And in all my years of experience, men don't like to use instruction manuals."

Mark looks at her with a grin and is about to say something when she cuts him off sharply.

"Don't you fucking dare."

His grin disappears immediately.

"I didn't say anything!" he says in mock protest and raises his hands in surrender. He looks back at me.

"Anyway, I forgot to ask, what was wrong with the

engines? It didn't seem to take all that long to fix in the end."

"Oh yeah, Robert seems to think that it was sabotage. I think I agree with him. By someone who knew what they were doing. Turned out to be a spoon shaped piece of metal purposely lodged between the plasma thing and the other bit next to it," I say, not really thinking.

Mark stands up fast, with an expression of disbelief and horror on his face.

"You mean one of us is a saboteur?" he asks.

I hadn't thought of it that way, I had sort of gone along with Robert's idea that whoever did this was on board the hangar section. One of us? Really? I know it definitely wasn't me, and suddenly that's the only thing I'm sure of now.

"I don't think that's very likely," Kerry says and puts her hand on Mark's shoulder and he slowly sits back down.

"None of us is smart enough to know how to stop the engine working without completely knackering it up for one thing, not even Robert, bless him. And it was me who suggested he look there in the first place."

"We don't know anything about Tim," I add, feeling slightly guilty.

"True," she says. "But we don't really know anything about this situation either. Other than the fact that our opposite shift has gone missing.

Presumably they're on the hangar, and that's done a runner too. Oh, and our engines have been sabotaged. Actually, when you say it out loud, it sounds fucked up enough to start a full on mass panic."

She pauses, scrunches up her face and looks upward for a few seconds and then continues.

"You're right though, John, we know nothing about any of the dump techs we get, we assume they're vetted in some way before they come aboard, but ultimately we don't know who they are, and never really know until we set out."

There is a silence as we all think about what she's just said. I don't know anything about Tim, except that he's really eager to please, very well presented, and doesn't seem to like Robert very much. Which kind of puts him in my good books if I'm honest. As far as I can tell, he doesn't come across as a saboteur. But then, I don't know how a saboteur is supposed to come across. If he has done this for some reason, I'm pretty sure he's not going to just admit it, so there isn't really any point asking him. But what other option would there be? There are no weapons on-board, so the only option would be threatening to blow him out of an airlock. I don't think any of us could do it. I certainly couldn't. On paper, we're pretty much the worst shift in the company, I've seen the graphs. We get by on the fact that our opposites are quite a lot better at their jobs than us, so we don't have to do very much. Anyone could have pulled one over on us and we wouldn't even have noticed. It's more likely that everything that has happened so far, has happened because the other shift wanted it to. That idea sort of clicks into place in my head, and seems to fit the situation quite nicely. Nicely, but it's also quite terrifying. I thought maybe they were trying to save the day, maybe being a bit selfless, heroic even, but the sabotage completely fucks that theory.

Tom has had a massive problem with us for a while now, and he constantly files reports on us when we get back to the Moon depot. Nothing is ever done about those reports. As long as the job gets done, Mr. Hooper doesn't seem to give a flying fuck. I've heard it drives Tom mad. That's only on the grapevine obviously, no actual evidence to back that up, just whispers and gossip. He's always quite nice to me face to face to be fair. But he knows we're really not up to the task. Hell, even I know that. But is he pissed off enough with us to leave us out here? It's possible I guess.

The more I think about it, the more it kind of makes sense. The only way we've got out of this so far was by an event that usually wouldn't happen in a million years. Robert actually listening to something that Kerry had suggested. I'm pretty sure now that Tom and his shift have set us up, and have left us out here to die. Or at the very least make us look incompetent enough to get us all sacked. That probably makes the most sense. But by sabotaging the engines while the ship was still cruising on its own inertia towards the sun they would have ultimately got us killed. Holy fuck, they were trying to kill us.

I look from Mark to Kerry.

"There's nothing to do now but wait for the proximity alarm to go off when we close in on the hangar. You guys may as well get some food, or something," I say.

Mark walks up to me.

"I'm not going to be able to eat anything, I'm a little bit freaked out at the moment," he says, wide eyed.

Kerry moves close, and speaks in a slightly hushed voice.

"What are we going to do about Tim then?" she asks.

I rub my face, not really knowing if it's a good idea to mention my newly formed and slightly flimsy theory about Tom and his shift. But I guess it'll stop any sort of confrontation with Tim, and that would make my life a little easier at the moment.

"In all honesty, I don't think Tim's done anything. I'm seriously beginning to believe that maybe Tom and his missing crew are responsible for this. Not in a saving the day kind of way. I think he's definitely onboard the hangar, but I think he sabotaged us, and was going to leave us out here to die."

Kerry is just about to speak up when we hear footsteps climbing up the ladder. Tim's head pops up and he looks at me. He's about to talk when instead he looks at Kerry and Mark. Both are staring intently at him.

"Everything alright up here? Do any of you need a drink or anything?" he asks slowly, looking slightly uneasy.

No one says anything, and the silence is starting to get a bit loud. I say the first thing that comes into my head.

"They're just freaked out because of the sabotage thing."

His eyes widen.

"What sabotage thing?" he asks.

I suddenly realise I haven't told him about it either, and feel like I've kind of put my foot in it. He does need to know, so better late than never I suppose.

"Oh bollocks, yeah, it looks like the engines were sabotaged."

I'm about to mention to him that I think Tom's shift is responsible for the sabotage, to make him feel more at ease, and spread my theory as far and wide as possible. But I realise that will do the exact opposite, and probably freak him the fuck out as well as Mark.

"Did you find out anything in the cargo bay?" I say quickly.

Tim shakes his head.

"Nothing seems amiss down there from what I could work out. I entered my access codes, and it just buzzed at me. According to the computer, nothing out of the ordinary has occurred. Everything seems to be how it's supposed to be."

He climbs out of the hatch and walks over to the thick book on the console table and rubs his hand on it.

"You don't see too many old books like this around nowadays, especially ones that big, what is it?" he asks.

"Oh, it's for when we catch up to the hangar. None of us has any idea how to link back up with it, so I thought I'd get the instruction manual out. I doubt it's been used for years. But it should hopefully have a guide to all the functions on the ship," I reply, sounding as upbeat as I can.

"I thought all that info would be on the computer," Tim says, and starts to flick through it.

"You'd think so, but no. The boss is way too paranoid about getting information stolen to allow us to put anything useful on there."

"No, he's probably right," he agrees absently.

Kerry walks to the ladder, and starts climbing down.

"I'm gonna get a coffee and some cake. Cake is best thing for a fucked up situation like this. No, two cakes. Maybe even some chocolate," she states, and then vanishes down the hatch.

I realise that I haven't eaten anything yet today, and notice that I'm sweating slightly and have a slight case of the sugar shakes. Chocolate does sound like a good idea. I follow her down, but stop before my head goes under the deck.

"Tim, when you've finished flicking, can you bring the manual down to me on the rec deck?" I ask.

"No worries, I'll be right with you," he replies, but doesn't look up and continues to flick.

8

I climb down the ladder, and Mark follows me briskly, leaving Tim alone on the bridge.

Kerry, Robert, Mark and I end up sitting on the table that's closest to the pool table, each taking one side of it, and all facing each other.

"How are we going to deal with this ... situation then?" Kerry looks and sounds like she may be a little bit on edge. Usually out of all of us, she's the hardest to fluster, she'll shoot you down first. But I'm beginning to see tiny cracks in her armour.

"I assume you're talking about Tim?" I say quietly.

"Of course I'm talking about fucking Tim! Who else could I be possibly talking about?" she whispers loudly.

I'm guessing the cakes haven't helped her with the

fucked up situation this time.

"I really don't think there's a situation with him," I say.

"So you're sticking to your half arsed theory about Tom and his crew? Do you realise how fucking stupid that sounds?" she says, and seems annoyed with me for suggesting it in the first place.

"It's the only one that makes sense to me. I know for a fact that Tom is actively hostile towards us behind our backs." I didn't really know that.

Mark looks up toward the hatch to the habitation level and bridge.

"Why have we just left him up there? He could be doing any number of sinister things," he says in a slightly hushed voice and points upward.

"I assume you and Kerry both logged out of your stations?" I ask.

They both nod their heads.

"He can't be then, can he?" I say and hold out my hands to make a point.

Robert joins in.

"Look, I agree that Tom doesn't really like some of us, and I agree that he is trying his hardest to get some of us sacked, but that really isn't motive for leaving all of us marooned out here. Tom's asked me to be on his shift loads of times, he's well aware that Sam doesn't know what she's doing. I've only said no to him because of my loyalty to this shift. He certainly wouldn't have left me out here to perish."

What a load of bollocks.

"Tim is the only suspect as far as I'm concerned." With that he folds his arms.

"Could this not be some sort of misunderstanding? You know, maybe something has been missed?" Mark says and looks hopeful, and then lowers his head slightly. "No, I guess not."

"Look John, I'm with Robert on this one. Even with the shit about Tom wanting him on his shift," Kerry says, sounding now like she's annoyed that she's ended up agreeing with Robert.

"Fuck you Kerry, Tom did ask me. He's asked me loads of times. Sam is useless."

"Look, stop arguing, I'm on your side you stupid fat fuck."

"Shut up, all of you," I say. "What do you want me to do? There's no evidence. Not for anything, either side."

"We could have some sort of trial, maybe," Mark sheepishly pipes up.

I look at him. I'm not sure what to say, it's beyond stupid. We need to be working together, not fanning the flames even more.

"We're not having some sort of half arsed trial, Mark," I say flatly.

"I think we should. I think Mark's right," Robert says and smiles.

"Really? How exactly are we going to proceed then, Robert? Bring him down here in irons? Sit him down and charge him? With what exactly? Who's going to be the judge? Who's fucking impartial enough to be the judge for that matter?! Then what are we going to do? What happens if you find him guilty? What happens?! This is ridiculous. You're fucking ridiculous."

"I think I'd be qualified to be judge, and he'd be judged guilty," he says and smiles.

I look down at the scratched surface of the table for a few seconds, and all my senses seem to go numb. I stand up and walk around table towards Robert, I can feel the eyes of every one looking at me, except for Robert, who's still smiling and looking at Mark. In one swift motion I punch him as hard as I can. In the ear.

It's enough. He cries out and falls off of his chair and onto the floor with a loud thump. I don't know what comes over me next, but before I realise I'm doing it, I'm kicking him again and again in his fat gut. I stop as I suddenly come to my senses, and stand back from him. The room is dead silent. I look around, Kerry and Mark both have their mouths open and are staring at me. Very slowly Robert starts whimpering. It's an awful, pathetic sound, and I start to feel terrible. It gradually gets louder until he's fully bawling his eyes out. He's curled up in a ball, and his whole body is heaving in time to the cries. His eyes are full of tears, and I can see a bubble of snot come out of his left nostril and pop. I'm a little bit ashamed of myself.

Kerry looks at me with wide eyes, I can't gauge her facial expression until she shouts at me.

"What the fuck?! Seriously! How's this going to help anything?!"

She stands up and pushes me backwards hard, and I almost lose balance. She stops, holds her hands open in front of her chest and tries to compose herself, and then sighs. She puts her hands together and looks at me, her expression now more one of a concerned mother.

"John, I'm sorry, I didn't mean that. But fuck, did you really have to start kicking him? I know a lot's happened today, but my god ... John, we've still got hours to go until we reach the hangar bay, it's probably best if you just fuck off for a bit, while we calm this shit down."

I don't say anything, only nod slightly at her and head to the ladder. I decide to go to my quarters, I think I need a bit of time alone before I talk to anyone again today. Part of me feels pretty good about what has just happened, I guess that'll be the kick of adrenaline, but that's fading fast now, and the feeling's turning to nausea. I wish I could embrace that part of myself sometimes, without the come down, without all the self-doubt, just go with it and see where it takes me. It probably wouldn't be anywhere good. And I realise that I'm glad of the nausea at the pit of my stomach. It was this part of myself that fucked everything with Ez, even though she doesn't know it yet. I'm sure her family do by now.

I open the door to my quarters and slam it closed for no good reason. I go over to the sink and run the cold tap, cup my hands under the flowing water and splash my face a few times. I pick up a towel from the floor and dry my face, then drop it back where it was. I kick off my shoes and lay down on the bed, and stare up at the grey ceiling. I notice a spider web in the corner, and begin to wonder how the spider that created it managed to get on board. There are too many possible reasons for this. Has it been here for years? Or did it hitch a lift on me from the Earth or the Moon? Maybe it got on board when the ship was built. What was that, thirty years ago? Do spiders live for that long? I doubt it. For fuck's sake, spiders are the last thing I should be thinking about. I'm in limbo. I'm between two places, neither of them good. I'm not supposed to be here, the events of today have managed to keep me focused on other things, and well away from the reason I'm not still back on earth. But it doesn't change the fact that I shouldn't be here anyway. I ... we had plans.

9

"Why am I wearing a purple tuxedo?" I ask Jacob. "I don't ever wear this sort of thing, I look like a fucking idiot."

"Then we'll all look like fucking idiots. But there's no way we'll get in wearing anything less," he replies.

"Get in where? Why won't you tell me?" I look to Terrell for some sort of support but he just smiles and looks absently upwards. I guess he knows everything.

"John, we're taking you to the ball," Jacob finally says.

"Why in the name of piss are you taking me to a ball?"

"Not *a* ball, John. *The* ball," he says and smiles.

"Okay then, let me rephrase: Why, in the name of piss are you taking me to *the* ball?"

"Because it's going to be fucking amazing that's why."

Jacob does occasionally have suspect judgement, but it always ends up being entertaining one way or the other. I look at myself again in the full length mirror on my wall, actually the tux does look pretty good. And together we do look like we might just fit in to any sort of upper class do.

"Sold. Who's ball is it?" I ask. Jacob and Terrell look at each other conspiratorially.

"It's the *Skylark* ball. At the city hall," Terrell says.

"That's the one with all the government officials, and everyone's a way higher class than us right? How did you manage to get tickets to that?" I ask.

"Very cleverly," Jacobs says. Terrell looks at Jacob, then at me.

"We're gate crashing," he says quietly, then sighs.

"But gate crashing very cleverly," Jacob says and puts on a huge childish grin.

"Well, I should have known it wasn't going to be as simple as just having tickets."

The city hall is only about twenty minutes walk from my small flat, so Jacob manages to convince us to save money and take a leisurely stroll instead of calling a taxi. It's never very wise to walk outside at night in this area, but I've never been mugged or raped. But then again, I don't usually stick out like a sore thumb as much as I do now. It's around seven pm, on a Saturday night and the streets are in darkness except for the lights of the buildings from the second or third floor up. Most of the shop fronts are boarded up and covered in graffiti, and most of the street lights are smashed. The whole area is pretty much deserted of cars and people. Only the mag-lanes way above us are busy with taxis and buses humming along taking people to their favourite drink and drug holes.

"How do you live around here John? I'd be terrified to leave my flat," Terrell asks.

"You get used to it, I just keep myself to myself and don't make eye contact. That is if I have to go out. I don't really have to leave the building. To get to work, or see you guys I just take the elevator to the underground parking zone. Bruce is in his own lock up and that whole section has security," I reply.

Jacob pulls a face.

"That vehicle of yours is the stupidest thing I've ever seen. Why did you call it Bruce? Of all the idiot names." I'm about to respond when something smashes a few metres ahead of us coating the pavement in a bright red liquid that quickly bursts into blue flames. It stops us in our tracks.

We suddenly hear a lot of shouting and screaming and before we can do anything about it, a gang of about twelve men and women are surrounding us. I look around at them in the dark, all just silhouettes and I can't make out any faces. I hear a click, and one by one their eyes start glowing red. My heart starts speeding up.

"I think we should have got a cab," Terrell whispers.

One of the red eyed silhouettes moves forward.

"You've made huge mistake walking through our neighbourhood without bodyguards you posh pricks," she says in a thick, but probably made up accent. The rest of the gang start a slow chant of "posh pricks ... posh pricks ... posh pricks ... ," which I'm guessing is a tactic to scare us. It's working quite well. My heart is now racing, and I'm terrified.

"Now give us all your money and expensive items and we may let you walk away with only minor injuries," the apparent leader says.

"Fuck that," Jacob shouts at the girl as he pulls something out of his pocket. "Do you know what this is?" He holds up a small black cylinder with a red button on top of it. The girl doesn't move, and the rest of the gang move in slightly closer. "It's a mini E.M.P. device. It has roughly a ten metre radius."

The girl starts laughing.

"Do you really think you can scare us with something that'll turn our phones off?" she says and laughs again, the rest of the gang start to laugh with her. It seems very forced.

"No, I was thinking more of your ocular implants. If they were done on the cheap, which judging by the area you live in, they were, it'll blow the little cheap fuses in your stupid heads and either blind you, cause you severe brain damage, or, if they was *really* badly put in, instant death. All options sound good to me at the moment." The whole group moves back as one.

"You wouldn't dare, you'd be arrested," The girl says slowly, her accent seems to be disappearing. It's now Jacob's turn to laugh.

"Really? You're going to call the cops? On us? Three wealthy bachelors who have been attacked in a red slum area on their way to the biggest ball of the year, defending themselves from a gang of red-eyed fuckwits? We'd be heroes," he says and clicks the top of the cylinder. The gang run away in all directions. We head quickly towards the bright city lights before they decide to come back.

"Fucking hell Jacob, good job you had that thing. I thought we were dead," I say.

Terrell looks at him and squints his eyes. "We live together Jacob. I'm sure you would have told me if you'd somehow got your hands on a mini E.M.P. You'd be far too excited about it not to." Jacob puts his hand in his pocket and pulls out the cylinder again and presses the red button.

"You absolute fucking prick," I say. To get us out of a horrible situation, I'd be happy to have all of my electrical items fried, but as a quick demonstration of the device, I'm really annoyed by it. But out of the red button comes a pressurised spray, and I realise it's just his aftershave. He smiles.

"You fucking prick," I say again.

"A mini E.M.P? I doubt even Tommy could get us one of those. He has however, after I got Terrell to keep badgering him, got us some fake *Skylark* identification that should get us into the ball," he says and pulls out three small white rectangular pieces of plastic and clips them to our jacket's top pockets. He then pulls out three pairs of glasses and passes them to us.

"When we get there, just walk through doors, and past the guards. The glasses should fool the retina scans, and the clips should fool the guards. Once we're through, try to look either rich or like you work for *Skylark*." Terrell and I both nod, and keep up our fast pace.

Within two blocks, the transformation of the city is amazing. From dark, terrifying, desolate graffiti-covered streets, to a bustling bright metropolis full of people and noise. The city hall looms in front of us. It's a grand old building, only slightly spoiled by the multi-coloured spotlights shining on every window and ledge.

"Just follow me, and do what I do," Jacob says, and we do exactly that. We walk through the massive revolving doors into the giant foyer, and straight past the guards. Lots of red lights flash in our direction, and there are a series of quiet beeps. I think for a few seconds that we've been made, and prepare to run, but we're allowed through and Terrell and I slowly follow Jacob into the ballroom. My heart is in my mouth the whole time, I don't know what to expect when we get in there, but we're given glasses of champagne as we pass the ballroom entrance and on tables either side of the dance floor, any kind of food and drink you can imagine is exquisitely placed and decorated, and every sort of drug you could think of made to look like part of the decorations. Hundreds of impeccably dressed people are slowly dancing or sitting and staring upwards. I look up above the dance floor and there are hundreds of small blue and white balls floating around the ceiling forming a kind of giant snake that is doing loops of the room, in a figure of eight that seems to turn itself inside out with every change in the classical music. I'm a little overwhelmed by it all.

"This is the most ridiculous, and vulgar thing I think I've ever seen," Terrell says. "It's terrifying how much money these people have." With that, he puts his hand awkwardly through his Afro, walks over to a food table and fills a plate with a bit of everything he can find. I gulp down my champagne and follow him. I realise how cheap our tuxedos look in comparison to everyone else's in here, and hope no one else notices. I turn around to talk to Jacob and he's disappeared. I scan the room, and he's already at the far side of the dance floor holding court with a group of ladies. I tap Terrell's shoulder.

"Look at him go, we've only been in here ten minutes. Lucky fucker," I say, shaking my head.

"Luck's got nothing to do with it John, he just oozes charm." I nod in agreement, and grab a plate and fill it with all the most plain looking things I can see. I decide to avoid the free drugs on offer as I don't really want to draw any attention to myself. Terrell and I just lean against the table and eat while watching people do their thing.

"This time, I'm really not sure why Jacob's done it. There's not really anything to gain from being here. If the guards realise that we're not supposed to be here, it's six months in prison, no questions asked," I say, still feeling bemused and overwhelmed by the situation.

"Don't worry, Jacob always has an angle. This time will be no different. Trust me," Terrell replies with a smile.

I look at Jacob from across the floor, and he's leading a woman away in the direction of the toilets.

"Yeah, he has an angle alright," I say and put more food on my plate, stuff a roll in my mouth, and start to head for a recently vacated table. I turn to Terrell and gesture with my head toward it, when with a crash I bump into someone, and everything on my plate ends up over her expensive looking dress. She just stares at me with her piercing blue eyes. The last thing I wanted was to draw any attention to myself, but I've pretty much ballsed that up now. I want to say I'm sorry, but I'm completely flustered and when I open my mouth to say it, my half chewed roll falls out and splats on the floor. I want to run really badly, and I'm about to bolt, when she bursts out laughing and gives me her hand.

"I'm Ezmerelda Kowalski, and that is by far the most interesting thing that has happened to me all night." I stare at her dumbfounded. "And your name is?" She asks.

I slap myself around the face.

"John Farrow. I'm so sorry, I've totally ruined your dress."

"Don't worry, I can't stand dressing up like this. I'm actually glad in a way, it means I can leave early now. So, John Farrow, I've never seen you before, what department do you work for? Defence? Sciences? Who's your boss?"

I'm a rabbit in headlights. Completely unprepared, I decide to tell mainly the truth, just changing certain details if they come up. Short answers are the key.

"I work at the loading docks, Martin Hooper is my main boss, but I report to Simon Prelude." I then whisper in her ear, "He's a bit of a prick." Maybe she'll believe me if I add a bit of colour.

"I haven't heard of either of those guys. It is a stupidly huge company though. Are they here?"

"Um, no. They probably don't do social gatherings. What do you do? Who's your boss?" I ask, not really knowing why.

"I work for the science division, mainly on classified stuff. My boss is Rupert Rawling. He's over there, dancing by himself with a masquerade ball style mask on. Keeping a low profile, while not at all keeping a low profile." She then whispers in my ear,

"Recently, he's been at the brunt of some malicious rumours, people are saying he ... I don't really know how to put this politely, so I'm just going to say it. Don't judge me," she smiles. "Apparently he's been caught masturbating over some of the equipment in the lab." She then laughs, "I don't know why I'm telling you this, I don't even know you."

"Did he actually do it? I mean, you know, bang one out?" I ask, and Ezmerelda raises an eyebrow.

"No. He's one of the good guys, in a company full of bad ones."

"You don't have to worry about me, I don't even work for your company," I blurt out without thinking. She gives me a stern look, then smiles again.

"To be fair, I had kind of guessed that. Your cheap purple tux gives you away somewhat. How did you get in here? Actually, I don't care. Give me a reason why I shouldn't have you arrested." She looks at me with a half smile, half frown, and I can't tell if she's joking or not.

"Because pretty much everything I told you was true, I do work at the loading docks and my boss is Martin Hooper. I just work for *Sunspots Waste Disposal Inc.* and not *Skylark*."

"I've heard of them, do you work on their spaceships?"

"No. I work the forklifts that load all of the horrible nastiness into the containers that then go onto the spaceships. It's not great. Actually it's pretty awful, but it pays for my life outside of work. Just. In general, I try not to think about it." I look down, and shrug my shoulders.

"Okay, I won't report you. For now. But only because I'm going home, and because you're going to take me to dinner tomorrow night." I was not expecting that.

"Why would you want to go to dinner with me? I'm sure you could have your pick of men, look at you, you're one of the most attractive girls I think I've ever seen. In this room alone there must be a hundred more suitable candidates."

"That's why. You seem to undervalue yourself. And you come across as honest. Even though you clearly lied and cheated to get in here. I'll let that slide for now." She grabs my hand and writes something on it, then walks towards the exit. I want to follow, but decide to let her go. I don't want to look too desperate. I look down at my hand, and her number is literally glowing at me. That's going to burn like hell tomorrow, but I really don't mind. I turn around to talk to Terrell, but he's gone. I have a look around the room and spot him with the group Jacob was with, taking full advantage of his cast offs. I smile, and decide it's time to go home. This time I am calling a cab.

10

Indian food was a stupid idea. I love it, but without fail I always go for the hottest thing on the menu. I really don't know why I do it, I can never finish it, and it always gives me stomach troubles. It was however, the first on my list of about six different international cuisines when I called up Ezmerelda, and she apparently loves Indian food, so the list stopped there. I agreed to meet her at eight that evening at the *Bengal Bastard,* it's apparently one of the best Indian restaurants in the city.

I get to the restaurant a few minutes early, and the waiter points a scanner at my eye and confirms my table reservation with a slight nod. He leads me through the packed and slightly gaudy looking dining room to my table. He takes my coat and I order a litre of beer and sit down. I look down at my watch, it's now bang on eight so she's not quite late yet. I look down again, and it's one minute past, so she is late now. My beer arrives and I drink deeply from it. I look at my watch again, it's now five past, and I start to wonder if I told her the right time. Did I say half past? Did I say nine? Now I'm not sure at all. I figure that if she isn't here by quarter past, no, let's say twenty past, then I've probably just got it wrong. Or she's not coming. What if she's not coming? What do I do then? I guess I give Jacob and Terrell a call and see if they fancy dinner on me. I take another large gulp on my beer, and then try to catch the eye of a waiter or waitress to get another one and spot Ezmerelda being lead through the dining room towards me. She looks stunning, wearing a pair of long, bulky black boots, tight fitting trousers and a long jacket. I smile and wave my hand in the air to let her know where I am, and suddenly realise how stupid that is, the waiter is leading her here anyway. The waiter takes her jacket, she orders a large prosecco and sits down opposite me. She smiles, I smile back, and realise I have no idea what to say. My mind has completely wiped itself of all information.

After a long, and slightly awkward silence Ezmerelda finally speaks. "Are we just going to sit in silence or are you actually going to say something? A pleasantry, or something nice about what I'm wearing? Maybe even something about the weather. But something, anything would be good."

My brain slowly starts to reboot itself.

"Fair enough. If you really want me to say something about the weather, I will. It's a bit crappy if I'm honest. But you do look stunning this evening, really stunning. I can't help but wonder, why are you here? You could easily have blown me off and claimed it was the drink talking. Um, I don't mean blown me off in that way though." Oh fuck, why did I say that?

She shakes her head slightly.

"You're really quite awkward aren't you? You seem to have some self-confidence issues. You have it, but it's at your own expense. It's like you know the world revolves around you, but you really wish it wouldn't," she says with a half smile.

"I don't know what I'm doing most of the time, trying to have fun, and keeping the boredom at bay mainly, I think." I look down at the table, realising that I'm beginning to sound a little bit depressing. "Enough about me, what about you, Ezmerelda. You're a ... scientist?"

"Call me Ez. Scientist is probably too strong a word for what I do. It's mainly programming. I never know what I'm working on, just tiny sections of a larger whole. I could have a guess, but it's better to stay out of the loop with *Skylark*. I'm sure if I asked Rupert, he'd tell me, but I honestly don't want to know."

The waiter comes and asks if we'd like to order, I haven't looked at the menu yet, but there's no point. I know what I'm having.

"I'll have the super phal please, and a garlic naan." Ez looks slightly taken aback by my choice.

"Really?" she says. "Good luck with that."

"It'll be fine," I reply, reassuring myself as much as her.

"Just Bombay potatoes and pilau rice please." The waiter takes our menus and walks away, and Ez looks around the room.

"I love the traditional service you get here, it's so impersonal most places you go. Just choose what you want from a pad on the table, and a few minutes later it just pops out of the hatch in the middle," she says.

"It's fine if you're a bit awkward around strangers, have self-confidence issues and don't want to leave a tip. But you're right, this is better," I reply, and she pulls a mock offended face.

"I guess it depends on your mood. Are you making fun of me, John Farrow?"

"I might be. But just a little."

"Don't you think it may be a little bit early in our relationship for that? What makes you think I won't just walk out?" she says, and I'm not sure if she's now making fun of me.

"Then I think, that would be the end of that. I'm not even sure I'd even call you up to apologise. I wouldn't want to be constantly walking on eggshells around you," I say, more bluntly than I intend. She stands up, and starts to walk away. I've fucked it, why did I say that? I put my face in my hands and then hear her laughing. I lift my head back up and she's sitting back down.

"I wouldn't walk out for that, John. Don't worry, so far I'm enjoying myself. I'm especially enjoying making you feel more awkward than you already do."

The waiter arrives with the food and places it in front of us. It smells divine. Ez looks at my naan bread.

"Do you want to go halves on the naan bread and the rice?" she asks.

"Of course, no problem," I lie.

Once we've shared the bread and rice, I pick up my spoon and have a mouthful. For about three seconds, it seems quite pleasant, and I can actually taste some of the delicate flavours. For about three seconds. After that, it simply feels like someone is stabbing my tongue with tiny razor blades. I quickly grab my beer and finish it in one, and it temporarily takes away the pain, but it quickly comes back. I ask the waiter for two more, and take a bite out of my half naan which soothes my tongue slightly more. I'm already sweating. Ez looks at me and tries to stifle a laugh.

"Good, is it?" She can barely compose herself. I've got two options here, admit defeat, or eat it as fast as possible and hope that two litres of beer will kill it. Like an idiot, I choose the latter.

"Bloody lovely," I say, and start shovelling it into my mouth. The beers arrive by the time I've finished it, and I drink half of one straight down. The heat of the curry has left me really light headed. In a haze that almost feels drug induced, I hear Ez ask if I'm okay. I nod my head, and stand up quickly. Too quickly as it turns out. It feels like all of the blood has drained from my head and I lose balance, and fall onto the edge of the table, which flips over and throws everything that was on it across the room.

Everything goes silent. I look up at Ez from the floor, she's looking around the room with her mouth agape. She finally looks down at me with a blank look on her face, I'm on my back, half covered in table cloth, beer, and some of her food. I give her a childish grin, and accept now would be a perfectly good time for her to walk out and never speak to me again. But instead, Ez starts laughing. Almost hysterically. When she's almost stopped, she gives me her hand and tries to help me up, I grab it but she can't keep hold because my palm is slightly sweaty, and I drop back down and she starts again, which set me off. We're still giggling as we're escorted out of the premises and out into the night.

"Well then, Ezmerelda Kowalski, would you like me to walk you home?" I ask, and she smiles at me.

"Only if you don't mind walking for about ten kilometres. I live with my parents a little way out of the city."

"I'm not sure I'm quite willing to do that. I'll call you a cab."

"And like that, the evening's over," she says.

"You still want to spend time with me?" I ask, a little confused.

"I know a little spot down by the river, it's not too far from here. Come with me." Ez holds out her hand and I take it. She leads me through parts of the city I have never seen before, loud, vibrant and very rich. The city finally quietens down and we walk down some steep steps just before an old bridge, and down onto a tow path. We find a bench and sit down. The reflections of the city on the water are breath-taking.

"You want to know why I still want to spend time with you? It's because I've never met anyone quite like you, John. I could even tell that last night, you clearly didn't fit in, but you're refreshing, a change in my world. Everyone I've dated in the past has had too much money. That comes with the territory I'm afraid. My dad owns the *New White Star*, one of the larger of the space cruise line companies. These men claim they could give me anything I could possibly want, but they're ultimately bland and vain and want me as a prize. You have treated me like a person, and I haven't laughed that much in years. Now, you probably think that I'm a spoiled brat, who's just slumming it, but I assure you, that apart from living with my parents, I earn my own money and take nothing from them."

"I don't think that." I'm not sure what to think, but now seems to be a good time to move in for a kiss. I'm pretty bad a reading signs from women, and often in the past when I thought the time was right to move in, they'd just pull back and ask me what the hell I thought I was doing. Ez doesn't pull back. After about a minute or two of passionate kissing, I pull back with the biggest grin on my face.

"Shall we go back to yours?" she asks. After what she's just said, the last thing I want to do is take her back to my place.

"That sounds great, but … my flat is in a red slum area, and I'd be slightly embarrassed to take you there on a first date. And besides, it's a terrible mess," I say.

"That doesn't bother me, after what I just said, why would you think it would?"

"I don't think it would. It does though, bother me. I can't let you see it just yet. I know that's odd, and probably a bit suspicious now I think about it, but it's not in a state to be seen by anyone who doesn't already know what it's like."

"You mean like your friends at the ball?"

"I've known them for years. A lot of the mess is probably down to them."

She stares into my eyes.

"You're full of surprises, John. You've pretty much just turned down a night of wild passion."

"I have, yes. It's probably because I'm a fucking idiot, and seem to do everything I can to sabotage myself."

"Maybe, but like it or not, you've just won me

over."

We slowly walk back to the bright, buzzing centre of the city hand in hand and head towards a taxi rank. We pick the taxi at the front of the queue, and the door raises open.

"Call me tomorrow," she says and gets in.

"Definitely," I reply and smile.

The cab raises from the road and attaches itself to the mag-lane high above, and with a loud whoosh it's gone. I'm now feeling at a bit of a loss. Did that go well? I'm not so sure now. It felt like it did, but I've been wrong before. Doubts start shooting through my mind, and I feel like I need to talk to someone about it. Jacob's mother has an open invitation to come and talk anything over and have a drink anytime any of us need to, so I decide to do that.

11

To my genuine surprise, Ez was still talking to me and within about two weeks we were an official item. The first few months together we pretty much did what all new couples do constantly. It was fantastic, and I've never been so happy. We didn't rush into anything, we just had fun.

When we'd been together for a year or so, we decided to move in together, and I'd insisted that we move into my flat, which I'd had now for around fifteen years at this point and I could never see myself moving out of. I honestly didn't think she'd go for it because of the area it was in. It's also full of all my old junk, and I had sort of got everything where I wanted it. From my point of view at least, I thought sharing it was a massive step. The view outside of the dining room and living room windows was of both levels of the M4, and there were talks of building a third level. If that happened, it would pretty much block out all the sunlight coming in. I didn't have a problem with this, as the curtains were mainly always closed anyway.

After a while of living together, we started having discussions/arguments about moving into a bigger place, and me getting a better job. Working forklifts on the loading docks at *Sunspots Waste Disposal Inc.* was pretty shitty, but it was pretty cool knowing everything I was loading into the square metal containers was headed for the Moon, and then on to be burned up in the Sun's atmosphere. But apparently, now, that lacked ambition. I was kind of comfortable with it, and enjoyed my life outside of work a lot. I didn't really want a career, and enjoyed spending a lot of my free time with Jacob and Terrell. Ez had worked really hard to get where she was, and had every right to try and push me into bettering myself. I just didn't really want to be pushed.

One day with a slight hangover, during my lunch break I get called into the manager's office. I'm annoyed that this had happened during my free time, and I'm quite happy to tell Simon this, even though I've probably been called in for some sort of reprimand. All Simon seems to care about is letting you know he's more important than you, and that he has the power to sack you. He's a slimy fucker and he looks like a stick insect. I knock on the door, hear the latch beep, and walk in. I'm ready to say my piece when I notice a large bald man in a cream coloured suit sitting to Simon's left. I vaguely recognise him, but can't quite place him. He stands up and offers his hand. I automatically take it, and shake it with a firm grip like I'd been taught to do from a young age. *"No one likes a limp handshake,"* my dad would always tell me. I didn't like handshakes at all, firm or limp. His hand is sweaty and all I want to do is wipe it on my trousers, but I manage to stop myself.

"I'm Martin Hooper, you must be John Farrow?"

The owner of the company. Fuck. I must have screwed up pretty badly this time for him to be here.

"I'm ... pleased to meet you," I say very quietly.

"Good, good," he booms. "Now let's get straight down to business, *Sunspot 2* is down a shift manager since Perry went missing a week ago. She's due to go out in four days, and I want you to take over."

I stare at him with my mouth slightly agape, I really don't know what to say. I don't know much about the business except for my job, I know that we have two ships and what they're called, and know that they dump rubbish on the sun, but that is pretty much all.

"It's double the money you're on now, and you'll basically be the captain of a spaceship."

"I'll have to speak to my girlfriend," I manage.

"There's nothing to talk about, man. Just say yes! I'll sort all the paperwork out, and arrange you passage on a shuttle to the moon depot tomorrow. From there you can start some basic training."

"Why me? I'm sure there are loads of more qualified … ."

He looks at Simon with a big grin on his face and bangs him on the shoulder a few times.

"Simon's told me nothing but good things about you boy, good things. I'm taking it as a yes, and will send the transport info to your house later today."

"Okay … thank you?"

With that he stands up again, walks past me and bangs me on the shoulder and leaves the office. Simon smiles at me, in a way that looks more sinister than happy.

"What's going on, how did this happen? I wasn't looking for this, any of this," I say, protesting, but knowing I'm going to end up doing it.

"Simply put, he can't find anyone else. He's tried, but no one wants the job."

"I don't want it either. Well, I don't not want it, but it's not something I've ever really thought about doing. Being a spaceship captain does have a certain appeal though."

"You won't be the captain. You'll be a shift manager. Simple as that. No one will ever call you captain. Look at it this way, the boss thinks you've said yes. If you let him down, you won't have a job." He pauses. "Look, from your position, you're getting a promotion because of a problem. From my position, I'm getting rid of a problem by a promotion." He leans back on his chair, puts his hands behind his head and looks really pleased with himself for what he's just said. I bet the fucker's been working on it all day. I do feel a bit gutted though. But still, it's a promotion. Whether or not I've earned it, or been forced into it, I'd imagine Ez will be pleased. Probably.

"So you didn't heap me with praise to Mr. Hooper then?"

"Oh I did. Lots and lots." He smiles an evil little smile. What a cock.

"I think you should go home and tell your girlfriend the good news, and start packing."

I stand up and head to the door. He stops me.

"Oh and John, here's the best bit, you're going be out there for three months."

My face drops.

Three fucking months. How am I going to explain that to Ez? And on such short notice?

I clear out my locker of everything that's of value to me and I walk out onto the yard. I watch everyone I work with doing their jobs for a few minutes from a distance, and I decide to disappear without saying anything. Mainly because I don't have any idea what to say to them. I quickly get into Bruce, my electro scoot, and head back home. Even in the awkward situation I've been put in, and potential falling out I'm going to have with Ez, when I get in and close the door, just for a moment, I can forget everything. I love Bruce. I've never been so happy with a purchase. He's a one person car, and looks something like a large bobsleigh, but with a roof. The best thing about this particular model is that if you want to go somewhere with someone else- assuming they have one as well- you can sit two of them side by side, hit the *connect* button on the key fob, and the two electro scoots do their thing and join together, syncing all systems and you have yourself a two seater. You can do this with up to four of them, but I couldn't convince either Jacob or Terrell to get one. It's embarrassing enough that I own one, apparently. Luckily, Ez does quite like them, and has called her's Brucette.

I head to my local pub *the Fire and Water* to have a sit down and a long think, aided by as much alcohol I think is necessary to sort this situation out. Ez meets me there when she's finished work, which is around three hours after I got there. By this point it's fair to say I've had a few. She sits down next to me and kisses me on the cheek.

"Hello, you here by yourself?" she says and looks around, I guess she's expecting to see Terrell or Jacob around somewhere.

"Afraid so." I look at her and smile. "They've given me, no, they've forced a promotion on me at work. I'm not sure I'm happy about it," I slightly slur.

She looks at me quizzically.

"Not sure you're happy about it? Why not?"

"Look, I know you want me to progress, and get a better job, and earn more money and all that, but it's not what I want to do. I like my job as it is."

"No you don't."

"No, I don't. But they've forced me into it," I say the last bit slightly higher pitched than the rest, and I realise that everything I've just said is complete nonsense.

"I assume by that you've accepted it then, this promotion that was forced on you."

"Yes, they said if I didn't take it I wouldn't have a job. So I had to. And now I'm on double the money, and…"

"Double the money? That's fantastic," she says and gives me a hug, and kisses me on the lips.

"Drinks are on you then," she smiles, then pulls back a bit when she notices I'm not entirely smiling back at her.

"Oh, I thought you were playing with me. You're really not happy about this? What is it they're *forcing* you into doing then? I assume some sort of management position at the yard?" she asks.

"Yes and no. Management, yes. At the yard, hell no."

"Tell me then, don't just string me along," she says, sounding annoyed.

"They've made me shift manager on one of their two waste disposal ships, *Sunspot 2*. And they want me to go out tomorrow for some basic training."

"What's wrong with that? It sounds pretty good. My boyfriend the space captain. How long will the training last?"

This is the part I was dreading, the part I needed three litres of beer for, and still I feel unprepared.

"The training will only be for a few days, but when it's over I'll already be on the moon depot and we'll be setting out straight away."

"So how long will you be out there for?

I wait.

"How long?" she says impatiently.

"Three months."

She stares at me, and then looks at the table. She doesn't move for a while, so I put my hand on her shoulder. She shrugs it off, and then just stands up, and walks out.

I don't see or hear from her again until I get back from my first three-month stint. I tried and tried to call her from *Sunspot 2* until the signal craps out near Venus, and then again when we get back in range on our way home but she doesn't answer.

After an uneventful first three months I finally get back to my flat. I unlock my front door and walk in. I'm surprised to see my flat in such tidy state, I hadn't emptied the bins before I left, so I was at least expecting the rancid smell of that to hit me when I opened the door. But no, it smells fresh like it's only just been cleaned.

I drop my bags in the hall and walk past the

kitchen into the living room. Ez is sitting on the sofa watching the holobox. She looks at me and stands up. She takes me in her arms and squeezes me tight.

"I'm so sorry for walking out like that," she says, and with that presses her head into my chest and cries. I hold her, and play with her hair.

"It's okay, it's okay, we'll figure this out."

And to a degree, we did. Everything seemed new again. After a lot of discussion, I reluctantly agreed to sell my flat and we bought a house, a modest three bedroom in a relatively nice area. Somewhere Ez could at least bring her parents. As a bonus, there was no three level motorway in sight, from any window.

Then came the first of many talks about children. In our early days we were both resolute in not wanting them. She was building a career, and I simply didn't want any. Something had changed, and I couldn't put my finger on what. All I knew was now, for some reason she wanted them, and I still didn't. That was that as far as I was concerned. Apparently that wasn't that, and the debates got more heated.

Every time I was leaving for *Sunspot 2*, we seemed to have an argument about it, and I was left to stew for three months. I guess we both stewed. It was always when *Sunspot 2* was closing in on the point of communication blackout that we seemed ready to talk about things again like adults, but then Venus happens and that's it for pretty much a month. When I got back, things always cleared up and we seemed happy again. The arguments always started again around about two weeks leading up to me leaving.

When I got back from my last trip to the sun, things were different. Ez had convinced me to hand in my notice, due to her bonus and promotion, and I did. The boss was not happy, and offered me loads more money to stay, which was very tempting. But I explained to him that the shifts were destroying my personal life, and money wouldn't change that. He seemed okay about it, but said he'd keep the position open for me as long as he could. I suspected he knew he couldn't get anyone and hoped I'd have a change of heart. Things were actually looking good for a change. It didn't take long though, for everything to completely fuck itself up.

12

There's a knock at my door.

"Go away," I shout, I'm not interested in talking to anyone, I'm quite happy being alone and miserable.

The door opens anyway, and it's Kerry.

"Have you calmed down yet, Mister fucking fisticuffs?" she says with a grin.

"Yeah, pretty much. I've just been day dreaming for the last hour or so. I honestly don't know what came over me, he's been trying to get under my skin ever since I started here. I think he may have just pushed me too far this time. What's happened anyway? Did you have your stupid trial?" I ask.

"No, and it wasn't my stupid trial. Robert is sedated in the sickbay. I think you may have broken a rib or two, you feisty fucker. Getting him up the ladder was a pain in the fucking arse. Have you ever tried to get a twenty stone blabbering fat man with broken ribs up a ladder? Jesus. After we managed that, I politely asked Tim to stay in his quarters until we reach the hangar bay. He seemed fine with it, and he just went. Odd bod, that one. Best leave him be until we've sorted this out I think," she says.

"Do you still think he's responsible for our dilemma?"

"I don't know, fuck, neither do you, John. In about three hours we'll find out, and one of us'll look like a prick. There was something else though, when we finally managed to get Robert up the ladder and in the sickbay, and got Tim in his quarters. Me and Mark decided to look at your instruction manual, you know, to see if we could get an idea about how to join up with the hangar bay."

"Fair enough, it's the only way to be sure," I say.

"Here's the thing though, the entire section has been ripped out. We had a hunt around your office, in your desk draws and in the cabinet. Couldn't find the fucker anywhere."

"Oh … that's pretty weird. Did it look like it'd been ripped out recently?" I ask, confused.

"How the fuck would I know? There's no way you can tell how long ago pages were ripped out of a book by just looking at them."

"Fair point, but that's really not good. How are we going to link up with the hangar bay?" I ask.

"When we get close, we'll slow the hell down and

hopefully some system will kick in and do it automatically. But the ship's so old that I doubt it's got anything like that. We're going to have to spend the time we have left looking for some sort of docking clamp control that no one has ever seen or noticed before, I guess."

"We're a little bit fucked aren't we?"

"That's an understatement, John. We are completely fucked."

"I'll go and look in the cargo bay, as that's got the only airlock to the hangar, it'd probably make sense that the controls to couple the hangar are in there somewhere."

She looks at me and smiles.

"Look properly this time."

I smile back.

"Fuck you," I say.

Kerry turns and leaves my quarters, I follow her. She heads up to the bridge, and I climb down to the rec deck, and walk through it towards the cargo bay.

Tim had spent time in here trying to figure out what had happened, but didn't have any luck, I doubted I would either. Although, if he was responsible for the situation, then he probably had enough time in here alone to cover his tracks. I walk up to the control panel next to the airlock, but slip on something before I get there. I find myself lying on my back on the floor again. The back of my head was still hurting from before, and now it fucking kills. It's pounding in time with my heartbeat. I sit up and look around for what it was I'd slipped on. It's a small patch of translucent slime, now smeared across the deck and on the bottom of my boot. I pull my finger through it, but there's not enough of it to give me a clear idea what it is. It's possibly the same as the stuff I slipped on in the inspection tube earlier. Strange, it has a similar texture to KY jelly, but not quite, it's more ... slimy, I guess. What is it then? I don't have time to consider it now, so I wipe it on my trousers again and stand up. Without thinking, I grab the DANGER: WET FLOOR sign that is propped up against the wall next to escape pod 1, and put it over the area where the slime is.

I then walk back to the control panel. I type in my password and it shouts at me again. I look around the door to see if there is anything else control like, and follow the wall down towards the outer doors for the escape pods. Nothing but pipes, piles of spare parts and bad lighting. This is useless, there isn't anything in here. I start back for the hangar bay airlock, when I look down and notice a small square area that's a slightly darker blue than the rest of the floor. It has four small ragged holes around the edge, and a larger hole in the middle, which has some cut wires protruding from it. Something has been removed. I kneel down to get a closer look, to see if I can work out if it's been removed recently or not. Not that I'd be able to tell, but I notice it has the same slime from next to the airlock and inspection tube all around it.

I'm suddenly worried. Is there something on board with us? I think about telling the rest of the crew, and then decide not to. I'd be laughed off the ship. After what's already happened so far today, it just isn't worth it. I think I may be jumping to some massive conclusions here anyway. But what happens if I don't tell them, and we all get killed by some sort of giant slime-dripping alien monster? I guess it wouldn't really matter because we'd all be dead. But at the same time, we'd be hailed as the first humans to discover and come face to face with extra-terrestrial life. That unfortunately went on to eat us. There's nowhere for something like that to hide on this part of the ship anyway, it's been searched level by level (badly) and I'm sure it would have been spotted by now. Unless it's a shape shifter … . Time to stop this stupid train of thought and get to the bridge and tell Kerry that I haven't found anything except wires protruding from the deck, where something, possibly the hangar release control used to be. I may omit the slime part.

I head back out to the rec deck and climb up to the bridge. On the way there I decide to get off the ladder onto the habitation deck and look in on Robert. I'm not sure why, I don't really want to say sorry to him, but I do feel crappy about literally kicking him when he was down.

I get to the door, which is slightly ajar and slowly push it open, it creaks on its hinges and I'm in. He's sitting up and watching something on the small old holobox on the wall. He notices me and flinches. He pulls the sheets up slightly. He actually looks terrified.

Guilt suddenly kicks in, and I automatically apologise.

"I'm really sorry, the um … stress of the situation?"

"Yeah … that's fine … we're all … um … ," he manages and trails off. He looks a little afraid, or maybe just a bit dopey from the sedative. He's breathing heavier and faster than usual and I'm pretty sure he just wants me to go, so I do.

"If there's anything I can do … ." I say.

"Okay … fine … ," He replies and quickly looks back at the box.

I walk out. That made me feel a little bit better.

I close the door behind me and decide to look in on Tim, maybe explain to him why he's been asked to stay in his quarters. He might be able to give me some perspective. I walk down the corridor and knock on his door three times. He opens it slightly and puts his head through the gap.

"Yes?" he says wide eyed.

"I thought we could talk, maybe have a hot or cold beverage?"

"Why would you want that? Judas," he says.

"What? No. What?" I'm confused. "I wanted to talk to you about … ."

"About why I've been confined to quarters? I

already know that. Kerry said you thought I was probably the saboteur. Which I'm not by the way, and that it was a good idea to stay out of your way until we reach the hangar bay and work out what's happening. I'd imagine that should be in less than an hour now."

Cheeky bitch.

"I don't think that, I never thought that. I was the only one who's had your back this whole time. But I suppose it probably makes sense for you to stay here, under the circumstances."

"Yeah, you guess. And I liked you." With that he moves his head back in and slams the door in my face.

That did not give me any perspective.

13

I walk back through the corridor and over to the ladder, I grab the rail and head up to the bridge. Once through the hatch, I quietly get up on to the deck. I stand behind Kerry and Mark for about twenty seconds before anyone notices me. Mark looks around.

"Oh, hi John. I didn't see you there."

"Hello," I say back. Kerry turns around on her chair.

"Did you find anything in the cargo bay?" she asks.

"No, it looks like there may have been some sort of control once, but it's been ripped out and only some wires are showing. By the way, I just spoke to Tim."

Kerry visibly tenses up and looks a bit sheepish.

"Didn't I say leave him be?"

Suddenly the proximity alarm starts blaring out, and the bridge's lights turn red. Kerry looks at me with an apologetic smile, and turns back to her console. I look out of the viewport and the hanger bay is pretty damn close now, and getting closer at quite a speed.

"Mark!" I shout through the blaring alarm, "I thought you said six hours? This hasn't even been five."

"That's what the computer said, we must actually be going faster than what we're rated at," he shouts back.

Kerry turns to him.

"Or the hangar is going a lot slower than you estimated. Either way, we have about ten minutes."

I put my hands on the back of Kerry's chair.

"When are you going to fire the retro thrusters?" I ask.

"When I'm good and fucking ready. Who's flying this thing? It's not you is it? It's me," she shouts.

I move my hands.

"Fair point, can you at least turn the alarm off then?"

The alarm turns off abruptly, and I end up shouting the last few words.

Kerry chuckles to herself, and turns back to me.

"Now Mister Captain sir, I shall fire the retro thrusters, and we shall slow down at your pleasure, if that pleases you. Then we'll prepare for fuck knows what."

"Thank you ma'am," I say.

She smiles and turns back around. She presses a few buttons on her console, waits a few seconds, then she tries the same sequence again, waits a few more seconds, and then re-tries it.

"What the fuck?" she mutters to herself.

I lean over her shoulder.

"Anything wrong?" I ask.

She continues trying the same sequence of buttons, and after nothing seems to happen a seventh time she bangs both of her fists on the console in frustration.

"Fuck, John, the retro thrusters' ain't firing, and we're too close to avoid a collision. We're going to hit the hangar at full speed in less than ten minutes."

Mark stands up, looking like he's going to freak out again.

"Sit down Mark, it'll be fine," I lie to him. He sits slowly, but I know what he's thinking. The escape pods are only two decks below us.

"Kerry, what would happen if we shut the engine off? With that piece of metal Robert found? Would that help?"

"No John, I've shut it down already. Without the retro thrusters' the inertia will carry us forward at the same speed indefinitely. And we're going pretty fucking fast," she says.

"Shit, we've got to think quickly. Um, where are

the thrusters' main controls, or how do we get to them?" I'm really not good at thinking on my feet.

"The retro thruster junction box is at the far end of the top inspection tube, where you were earlier. The fuel pipes to the thrusters' themselves are underneath the box, and made of rubber, and stupidly thin so it's possible for them to get easily blocked. It's a really, really dumb design, made worse by the amount of times it's bodged back together."

Oh bollocks. Can this be my fault? I'd forgotten all about dropping the spanner and it wedging itself between the fuel tank and what I thought were random tubes. No one told me to be careful of anything except for being electrocuted. It would have to be a really dumb design if a small spanner wedged against them could stop the retro thrusters firing.

"Um ... it's possible that I may have dropped a spanner in the gap underneath the box earlier. Could that have blocked the pipes?" I ask.

"You fucking idiot. That'd definitely do it, what did I just say? It's bad design. Why didn't you say anything about this earlier? And how did you ... oh never mind," she says, waving her hands in the air.

"I was trying to undo a bolt, Robert was being a prick, and the engines suddenly turned back on, in shock I dropped it. I thought I was going to get electrocuted," I say.

"Well then, in that case, you have about nine minutes to get the spanner out of there, or we're all going to die." She turns to Mark. "Get to the escape pods, and prep them for launch."

I turn towards the hatch, ready to get my ass to the engine room as fast as possible, when Tim pops his head up looking panicked.

"I noticed through the viewport in my quarters that we're not slowing down, why haven't you fired the retro thrusters? Are we going to hit the hangar?" He says.

"Yes, I dropped something onto the thruster fuel pipes and now they're not working, I've got to get down there now!"

"I can do that, I've flicked through the manual and seen inspection tubes, and know where the retro thruster junction box is, and I'm nimbler on my feet than you."

"Okay, good. Fucking go, then!" I shout.

He slides down the ladder and I follow him, I look back at Kerry.

"You get to the escape pods too, and leave the thrusters controls turned on so they fire as soon as the tube is unblocked."

She nods, grabs Mark and they follow me down the ladder. I get into the engine room and Tim's already getting into top tube. I shout after him.

"If you're not at the junction box in three minutes, turn back or you'll be crushed. The top tube will be directly underneath the hangar deck when it hits!"

I climb up to the top tube and look in. He's making

really good time, he looks like he's almost halfway down the tube already. He shouts back at me.

"Close the hatches, just in case. You wouldn't want to be sucked into space if this doesn't work."

I don't argue, and shut all three hatches, but don't lock them. I don't want to trap him in there if I can help it. Selfishly, I decide to leave the engine room and climb back to the bridge and maybe watch the carnage from the highest vantage point. I reason that if he succeeds, all will be well and I won't be needed, but if he fails I don't want to be in the line of fire. The bridge is probably the safest place on board. We're heading towards the hangar bay from underneath, it should hit its housing first, which the inspection tubes run along the top of. All of that's all on the engine room level, at the bottom of the ship. Best case scenario if Tim fails, it may shear off the housing, taking the fuel tanks and some of the engine room with it, leaving us heading towards the sun with no fuel or power to stop ourselves. All other scenarios pretty much mean we die instantly. If we're going to die, at least I went down with the ship. As a captain goes down with his ship. As a shift manager goes down with his ship ... . Actually, fuck that. If I'm not the captain, then I mean to live.

I get off the ladder at the rec deck and run toward the escape pods in the cargo bay, hoping they haven't been launched already and find Kerry and Mark walking back in from the cargo bay.

She looks at me and shrugs her shoulders.

"Guess what?"

I look at her blankly.

"Neither of the fucking escape pods have had their oxygen tanks replenished."

I wonder briefly if it was my job to check that.

Suddenly, a countdown starts over the intercom.

"*Collision in sixty seconds.*" It states in a calm female voice.

"I think we should head to the bridge, it's probably the safest place on the ship if Tim fails," I say to both of them.

"*Collision in fifty seconds.*"

We all climb the ladder to the bridge, Kerry up front, Mark in the middle and me last, and I suddenly realise Robert has no idea what's going on. It's probably for the best, and there isn't really time to warn him now. Ignorance is bliss.

"*Collision in forty seconds.*"

We climb out of the hatch and stand on the deck of the bridge. We all stare at each other. Kerry then looks at Mark, grabs him and gives him a massive kiss. He kisses her back, not looking surprised by it.

"Have I missed something?" I say.

"*Collision in thirty seconds.*"

Kerry looks at me in disbelief.

"You really didn't know? Fucking hell. Really? Whenever you fall asleep in your office on shift, we pretty much constantly fuck."

"Collision in twenty seconds."

"I absolutely did not know that. I also didn't know you knew that I fell asleep on shift."

"Oh we did, but we didn't really mind," Mark says with a sly smile.

"Collision in ten seconds."

"Brace yourselves, this is it," Kerry says.

We all grab hold of the hand rails that are intermittently spaced on every wall, and hold on for dear life.

"Collision."

We look at each other, and for a moment nothing happens. I start thinking maybe it won't happen, maybe what we can see happening through the viewports isn't real, maybe the retro thrusters' have fired. Even then it would be too late, at the speed we were headed towards the hangar deck this late in the game, it would have made no difference. Kerry grabs hold of my hand. I look into her eyes, they are wide, but she is smiling. She looks like she has accepted the inevitable. Then it hits.

There is a massive low rumbling bang from beneath us, and the whole ship heaves, the three of us go flying forward. There is a horrible sound of grinding metal and smashing glass, sparks and fire start spurting out of the consoles. I get thrown into the pilot station, pain shoots through my back, and I can see flames and thick black smoke everywhere. I don't see where Kerry and Mark have ended up, but someone is screaming. I struggle to move, but I'm fading in and out of consciousness, I try to stand, but I fall to my knees, then everything fades to black.

14

"John, wake up! It's nearly eleven, you could win medals for the amount that you sleep."

I rub my eyes and see that Ez has a coffee in one hand, and some sort of healthy breakfast bar in the other. What I wouldn't give for a fry up right about now.

"I'll leave these here, but I want you up in ten minutes."

She puts the coffee and breakfast bar on the bedside table, smiles and leaves. I sit up, grab the coffee, and take a sip. Yuk. It either hasn't been stirred or there's no sugar. Oh well, even like this it's still better than anything on *Sunspot 2*.

Even though this would technically be my three month break now, knowing that I don't have to go back to that ship feels pretty good. So far though, I haven't spent the time wisely. I've spent the last month and a half since handing in my notice pretty much drinking with Terrell and Jacob every night until stupid o'clock in the morning. I think Ez is beginning to get annoyed by this, but so far she hasn't said anything. It's probably time I tried to get out of this cycle of drinking, and attempt to get a new job. One with fewer hours, and hopefully less pricks to deal with. I will miss Kerry though, but probably not enough to contact her again. Does that make me a bad person?

I down the coffee in one glug, then get out of bed. I put my dressing gown on and head downstairs.

Ez is sitting reading her tablet at the kitchen table, and it occurs to me that it must be the weekend.

"Good morning my little booze monster," she says, but I think I sense a hint of annoyance. "There's fresh … ," she looks at the coffee pot and pulls a slight face. "Fresh-ish coffee in the pot, if you want it."

I look at the pot, my mouth still tastes like crap from the drink last night and the coffee I've just had.

"I think I'll pass. Do you fancy going out and getting some breakfast?"

She looks at me, then at the clock on the kitchen wall, then back to me. "Breakfast?"

"Okay, lunch-fast? Or break-unch?"

"Yeah, sounds good. Do you want me to pair up Bruce and Brucette while you get ready?"

"I thought I'd left Bruce at the pub."

"No, he's where he normally is."

I'm a bit concerned, I'm sure I drove him to the pub. I don't remember how I got back last night, I really hope I didn't drive home in him. I'd be incarcerated for a full year if I'd have been caught, even if the Bruce was on autopilot. Hopefully the days are just blurring in to one, and I'm getting mixed up.

"I don't think you took him last night anyway, didn't Jacob pick you up?"

That was it. Thank fuck. I really need to stop drinking my head out every night, I'm really beginning to lose track.

"Can we walk? I don't think my stomach could cope with the journey."

"That's fine, we'll go to the cafe with the nice milkshakes. What's it called? You know … it doesn't matter, whatever it's called, it's the closest one."

The sun is way too bright for my hangover, but we're half a kilometre down the road before I even think about sunglasses. It's too late to go back, and my gurgling stomach is telling me that bacon is more important than vision at this moment in time. Strange how the sun seems less bright when you're right up close to it dumping waste materials.

Ez decides to take us down the path by the river, it'll add on a few minutes to our journey, but it is a lot nicer than walking next to the road, with the constant whooshing of silent cars speeding by, blowing you sideways. Ez sits down on a bench that faces the water, and beckons me to join her.

The glare on the water feels like it's burning out my retinas, and making my headache worse. As we sit in silence for minute or so, I start to get the feeling we're about to have a serious conversation. I'm not sure my brain is going cope.

"I love this spot. Everything always seems so tranquil. So quiet."

It is a beautiful spot, but I'm hungry and my head hurts. All I want to do at this moment is to keep moving until we get to the cafe.

"John, I know since I asked you to finish your job you've been a little … I don't know, what's the word … lost? I know you don't want to rely on me financially, and I truly get that. But for us to move forward, I needed you out of that awful job. The time we spent apart, it was just too destructive to our relationship. But now, since you've quit, you seem to be on a destructive path of your own. You're drinking every night. You really need to grow up, you're all nearly forty and you act like teenagers. I like Jacob and Terrell, I really do, but you're all bad influences on each other. I'm working my ass off to put us in a good position for the future, and you're just pissing it up against a wall."

It's all true, and I can't argue with any of it. I look out over the river, and then down to the gravel path, trying desperately to come up with a reason for why I'm doing this, why I seem to be rebelling against what should be a perfect life. But I have nothing. So I stay silent. She waits a moment for a reply, but when none is forthcoming she carries on.

"You know my boss? Well, I think you know him, Rupert Rawling?" The name rings a bell in my head.

"He's the one who was caught banging one out over the equipment right?" I say and smile to myself.

"Is that really the only thing you remember me saying about him?" she says. It was.

"He's a good man with a nice family, and someone decided to start some malicious rumours about him. I told you because it was funny and something he just wouldn't do."

"You've mentioned him loads of times, but I've never actually met him face to face."

"No, of course you haven't. You're always away on that ship of yours whenever we've had any work related social gatherings. Anyway, he's been acting really odd recently, and seems to be getting cold feet about the project we're working on. I don't know the full picture as I only work on small elements of it here and there. But he seems to think that the plug will be pulled anytime soon, and that we'll all be re-assigned. If that happens, I'm going to take some time off, and we can spend some proper time together. And maybe even think about the possibility of having children."

Alarm bells ring in my head. I sit up straight.

"We've talked about this a hundred times," I

say. "We're not having kids, I don't want them, and you don't want them. You said they'd fuck up your career."

"I'm at a really good point in my career at the moment, pretty much where I wanted to be at this age. Having a baby wouldn't ruin anything now, it would just put things on hold for a while. I could go back in where I left off, when I'm ready."

Here we go again. When did having children become such a priority for her? She used to be more adamant about it than me. I've stayed in the same position this whole time. I don't really want them. She seems to have gone from *No way, absolutely not, my career is far more important.* To *let's have babies, and fuck my career.*

"Ez. We have this argument almost every time I'm about to head back to the sun. It ends up with me being miserable and alone for three months, and I'd imagine it's similar for you. Except that you have friends to talk to, and I'm trapped on a tin can with a bunch of people I don't really like, and certainly don't want to open up to."

She looks at me for a few seconds, and then looks back out over the water.

"I guess that's true, I'd never really thought about it like that. But you're not going back this time, you're staying here. And to put it bluntly, you could easily be a stay at home dad."

I look at her sharply.

"Fuck that."

I realise that she has it all planned out, and probably has done for a long time. And now, finally all the pieces are in place.

"I'll let the idea sink in, and we'll talk about it again in a few days."

With that she stands up, grabs my hand and pulls me up. I'm feeling shell shocked and not sure I know what's going on.

"I think it's now definitely time for break-unch, or would you prefer lunch-fast?" she says, and I suddenly realise how ridiculous I sound.

"Um ... just brunch I think."

We head to the cafe in relative silence, not an entirely uncomfortable one, but my head is reeling. I'm going to need another evening with Jacob and Terrell to talk through the events of this morning, and to get their unique wisdom on the situation.

15

"Tonight my good friends, will be a night like no other. We won't simply be staying at our local *the Fire and Water* to whittle the night away, no, no, no. Tonight will be something very special indeed. For I have procured us three tickets to the finest drinking establishment in the city. The one and only *Jupiter Rising*. Ten floors of truly awful music, ten floors of watered down piss, ten floors of overpriced drugs, ten floors of terrible letching men, ten floors of buff, sexy men, and ten floors of sexy scantily clad ladies. Tonight my friends, we go into the realms of the unknown."

Terrell looks over to me and puts his hands over his face. I feel the same, *Jupiter Rising* is a shit hole of epic proportions.

"Really, Jacob? Why would you do that to us? This

is probably my last night out with you guys for a while, and we're going there. Really?" I say.

The waitress turns up and puts three litre glasses of lager on the table, looks at Jacob with a sneer, and walks away. He just smiles. The company logo on the side of the glasses is glowing red and slowly changes to blue when the tiny mechanism inside has chilled the drink sufficiently.

Jacob picks up his glass when it's ready and drinks deeply from it, then puts it down on the table loudly.

"That is precisely why, John. If it's our last night together, then let's do it with as little style as possible," he says.

"I get that, but I really have something serious I need to talk to you guys about tonight, I thought maybe a quiet one."

"John, three words are going to sum up tonight: Stupidness before seriousness," he says, and then holds his glass in the air.

Terrell picks up his drink, bangs it against Jacob's already half finished one, and takes a massive swig.

"Ah, fuck it. I'm in. Come on John, this could be the final chapter of the three musketeers," he says.

"The three musketeers? We've never called ourselves that. The three drunken bastards more like it." I sigh. "Okay, I guess I'm in. Not that I have much choice. We are going to regret this though." I bang my glass against theirs and attempt to down my drink. I don't even get to the quarter way mark before

I start gagging and spit a mouthful on to the table. Luckily, only Jacob and Terrell see me do this, otherwise we'd have probably been kicked out. The waitress was already annoyed with us, but she seems mainly annoyed with Jacob. He won't tell us why, but Terrell seems to think it has something to do with Jacob sleeping with her one night, and then sleeping with her boyfriend the night after. They still point at me and laugh.

After our drinks are finished, we leave a tip and Jacob books us a taxi to the club. We walk outside and the three of us wait in the rain shelter until the taxi decides to turn up. There are four large circled *T*s in what used to be the car park, and our taxi lands on the one closest to us. The side door hisses open and the driver shouts out Jacob's name. We get in and sit down.

"Here we go, boys, the point of no return," Jacob declares, and pulls out three mini bottles of something luminous and blue. He passes one to both Terrell and me and downs his in one. We look at each other and down ours too, as the glowing blue mouth effect it gives us only lasts about an hour, but is brightest ten minutes after you drink it. We're going to look ridiculous when we get there. But then, that's the point. Three old men entering a club that is predominately filled with eighteen to twenty five year olds with bright blue glowing smiles. We're so cool.

The cab then slowly moves itself into the mag-lane

ten metres above the road, and with a loud buzz that signals its roof is within the magnetic barriers, it heads off at full speed, and the backs of our heads hit the head rests. Only service vehicles are allowed the conversions needed to make them able to hover and use the mag-lanes. It makes taking a bus or a taxi a hell of a lot quicker than driving. Especially in the city. It does mean that bus and taxi drivers need special licences and a lot of training to pilot these vehicles, and has put most of the road based taxi drivers out of business.

Out of the window I spot the club between buildings that are blurring past at high speed. It's a huge tower covered in lights and screens, in the middle of an industrial estate. It looks out of place, and in the daylight just looks tired and old. It's a beacon for anyone who wants to dance, take its many varieties of mind altering drugs, have a one night stand, a quickie by the dustbins, or a fight. A classy place.

The taxi comes to a stop, slowly moves itself out of the mag-lane, and sets down about thirty metres from the club. The driver presses a button and our retinas are scanned with a bright red light. There is a fast beeping noise, and he acknowledges that we've paid by unlocking the doors.

16

The crowds outside the place seem to be as packed as the club itself is probably going to be, but there doesn't seem to be a queue. Each level has its own entrance, with avoids a lot of the congestion.

"Jacob, which one's the rock level?" I shout over the noise of people and thumping bass coming from above.

"Not sure, probably near the top I'd have thought. Not going there yet though, I've got a plan." With that he walks over to a water machine, and pulls out a litre bottle and proceeds to down it. He then walks to one of the bouncers and asks what level is generally the most popular.

"We're going to level four first." He smiles a sly little blue smile, and I think I know what he's planning. The three of us walk through the foyer and towards the level four stairwell. All the hip and sexy people seem to be headed this way too, and they all seem to have almost no clothes on. The men, tight shorts, naked torsos, and shimmering tattoos across their bodies and arms. Very in fashion right now. The women, essentially wearing just lingerie that has been repurposed as the standard nightclub uniform. There must have been a point sometime in the past when a mini dress just wasn't mini enough anymore. I'm not complaining though.

Once up the stairs, the muffled beat gets louder and I start to feel it in my chest, as if it's trying to change to beat of my heart. The crowd stops, and waits patiently at the giant doors willing them to open. When they finally do, the strobe lights floating just below the ceiling lead us in. The beat stops being muffled and becomes sharp, and almost intolerably loud. Jacob disappears in ahead of us, and Terrell taps me on the shoulder. He tries to say something to me, but I can only see his lips moving and have no idea what it is over the racket. He then drags me in the direction of the bar, and we get quickly stuck in the tightly wedged, claustrophobic mass of people waiting to be served. There is nothing to do now but wait and hope the bar staff don't just serve the people who show them the most cleavage.

Jacob then grabs us both by the shoulders, we turn and look at him, confused. By some miracle, he's already been served and managed to find us a place to sit. He definitely doesn't have the most cleavage, out of the three of us, that'd probably be me, but he probably has the most charm. Either way, that man works fast. Once we sit down, he puts the three *Emergency Stops* he's bought us on the table, and we all smile in unison. I'd forgotten that they served them here. I pick up the small yellow box, attach it to my arm, and wait for them to do the same. Once they're all in place, we count down from three, and then hit the big red button on the top. The needles inside the yellow box pierce our skin, and the modified opiates hit our blood streams. We all then lay back on the sofa, mouths slightly agape. My body feels really heavy, too heavy to move, and I feel like I'm floating at the same time. It's a good feeling. The effects will only last about ten minutes, and the addictive element has been removed, but the club will only serve you one per night. There are plenty of other ten-minute hits available, but four different hits is the limit for one person in one night. The owners of the club have to be super strict on this policy now, because the previous ones were just too relaxed about it. Jacob told me of one night, probably about a year ago, when a group of friends took it in turns buying as many as they could from the bar, and took them all at once. It was a terrible idea that ended very badly. Some of them got serious brain damage and had to be euthanised in the days following, and some just died on the spot after their brains literally melted and drained out of their ears and eye sockets. The owners of the club were promptly arrested, and executed soon after.

Once the effects of the *Emergency Stop* have worn off, Jacob stands up and tries shouting something at me, but I just can't hear him, so I point to my ears and shrug my shoulders. This place is horrible. I like being able to talk, and I've got a lot to discuss this evening. The repetitive pounding bass is getting in the way of everything, except drinking, drug taking and dancing. And there's no way I'm dancing.

He laces his fingers together and bends his knees, and I just look at him. I finally realise he's miming for me to give him a bunk up. So I copy his stance, and he runs at me. He lifts his leg and puts his foot between my hands. I push up while he jumps, and he grabs one of the floating strobe lights above us, and hovers slowly above everyone dancing and getting their groove on. I realise with horror that I may have just put his plan in motion.

He glides gracefully over the crowd and drops down when he gets near to one of the six or seven dancing poles placed around the room. The one he lands next to has no one dancing or writhing on it, and he walks towards it. He looks left and right, and then proceeds to climb it, and it looks like he's planning on climbing up as far as it goes. I turn to Terrell and motion towards the exit. He looks puzzled and raises an eyebrow, until I point at Jacob steadily making his way up the pole. He stands up quickly, nods his head, and we swiftly head for the giant doors. We work our way through the throng of sweaty semi-naked bodies writhing and grinding around us, and when we're within a few metres of the exit, we turn around to watch the carnage begin. If what happened next hadn't been so disgustingly horrible, it may almost have looked beautiful.

17

Jacob finally reaches the top of the pole, then crosses his feet and holds his knees together. He holds out both of his arms and begins to slowly lean back. When he's pretty much upside down he holds his position for a few seconds, and then pulls his arms back in. He then looks around the room, and spots Terrell and I by the doors and smiles. He then puts the fingers of his right hand down his throat. At the same time, he loosens his grip slightly on the pole and starts to very slowly move down it and spin around. He quickly withdraws his fingers and projectile vomits on the unsuspecting people underneath. This is no ordinary vomit mind you, this is bright blue, and glowing. He loosens his grip some more, and he spins faster around and down. It goes everywhere, a giant circle of luminous sick. The people dancing underneath look up, smiling, assuming it's some sort of special effect the club has put on, until they smell it. Then all hell breaks loose.

Jacob is down and running towards us before anyone's realised what's just happened. But he's making slow progress because of the crowd. I see a few people with glowing blue on their heads and shoulders point in Jacob's direction and start to give chase. From where he is, he raises his hands above his head and flaps them about in the universal *Run like fuck!* gesture. We don't have to be told twice. I turn to head for the exit as fast as I can, but before I realise it's happened, I smash straight into a massive guy carrying a large tray of drinks. The glasses smash, cutting his bare chest and the drinks go everywhere. His face goes from shock to fury in a split second. He then suddenly bangs the back of his head, his eyes start to glow bright red, and so do his shimmering tattoos. He grabs me by the throat and slams me against the wall, holding me so my feet are dangling above the floor. I can't breathe, and I actually think he means to kill me. Terrell tries to pull him off me, but one swipe of this guy's left arm knocks him on his ass. Black spots start appearing in my peripheral vision, and he moves his head closer to mine. I can see in his red eyes that he doesn't plan to stop this anytime soon, and he squeezes tighter. I try to hit and kick him, but he doesn't move. I just about spot Jacob still running towards us. He grabs a bottle from a table as he runs past it, jumps up in the air and smashes it on the back of the big guys head. His eyes open wide, and they change colour from red, to blue, to purple. It repeats the pattern, getting faster and faster. His eyes start strobing and he let's go of me and grabs the sides of his head. Sparks fly out of the back of his skull where the switch must have been and he falls to his knees screaming. The bottle must have damaged the switch, and whatever liquid was in it must have somehow got into the implants. Poor fucker. But that's what happens if you get ocular implants done on the cheap.

Jacob grabs Terrell and pushes him out of the doors, I don't hang around and leg it after them. I look over my shoulder as we're running down the stairs and can see three vomit covered people in pursuit. Adrenaline has kicked in and I can only just feel the pain around my neck. We get through the foyer a lot faster than I would have expected with the amount of people milling around and generally getting in our way, and then we're finally outside and into the cold wet night. We continue running and end up heading back towards the lights of the city.

We stop after about ten minutes when we realise that anyone who was chasing us has long since given up. I'm so unfit that when the adrenaline starts to wear off, the combination of being strangled and trying to catch my breath work against each other and the effort to breathe hurts so much I almost collapse.

After a few minutes of sitting down, I'm still wheezing slightly, but breathing fine.

"Jacob, you absolute bastard," I say. "You had that planned all night didn't you?"

"Everything except you getting strangled. The circle of blue? You know I've always wanted to try that, well ... ever since we came up with the idea and decided it wasn't possible. And I wanted your last night out to go with a bang. Did it look good from where you were standing?"

"It was the best, and worst thing I've ever seen," Terrell says, and then looks at me.

"What's the reason then? Why's this your last night?" he asks.

I look at the pavement, and am about to answer when we hear a familiar whirring noise.

"Stand up, and start walking," Jacob says, suddenly really serious.

We start walking and the police cruiser slowly moves past above us on the mag-lane. It slows down even more and shines its spotlight on us. We're so fucked. After what happened at the club, I'd be surprised if we didn't get electro-shock treatment to correct our behaviour, and then have to spend the next six months inside. I hold my hand to protect my eyes against the brightness, although that's the least of my worries now, when all of a sudden, it switches off. With a quiet hum, the police cruiser speeds away. The three of us stand dead still. We start to slowly look around, and then look at each other, and finally, we burst out laughing.

We continue walking, and the laughter subsides.

"John, I know this isn't actually your last night out with us, but you're not going to be around so much anymore, are you? It feels like maybe the end of an era, and I get the feeling you have something big to talk to about." Jacob puts his hand on my shoulder.

"But you know we can't do that without seeing my mother, and we're not far away, it's only a little way down the road from here."

When we were kids, Jacob's mother would always let us drink or do anything stupid at her house, she said that it was better to be supervised, that way we'd stay out of trouble and not get ourselves arrested. As we got older, she would often join us on our misadventures and I never really thought of her as Jacob's mother at all, just another friend. She always had the best advice, on most subjects, and was a great listener. She did have some odd quirks though, she was heavily into the idea of an afterlife, and spirituality, (whatever that was) even after the main religions had been abolished and such beliefs could get you arrested or put in an asylum.

We get to the gate. It's locked. We start to walk around the outside perimeter, and notice that there are some bent bars on the iron fence. We climb through and walk past the countless shabby looking graves, to the one that is still constantly tended to. Jacob comes here once a week, to think, and to maintain it, even though the rest of the place seems to be going to ruin. He made her a promise on her deathbed that if he had any big decisions to make, or any problems in life, he'd come and visit, and have a drink with her. And that offer had been extended to all of us. When Terrell split from his wife, we came here and had a drink with her. After my almost disastrous first date with Ez, I came here afterwards and had a drink with her. Maybe it's just the quietness of this place, or because of her strange beliefs somehow it feels like maybe she is still here and listening. But more than that, it always seems to help. She died far too young, and I still miss her.

Jacob and Terrell made a small, slightly shoddy bench to put beside the grave about six months ago, so we all sit down, and it creaks under our weight. Jacob pulls out four bottles of beer from his man bag. He passes one to me and Terrell, and puts the forth one in front of the headstone.

"What's going on then Johnny boy?" Terrell asks me.

"Everything. Nothing." I try and think of the best way to say it, but decide that straight out with it is probably best.

"Ez wants kids. After years of not wanting them, she now does. She's made me quit my job, and has said she wants me to be a stay at home dad. I really don't feel grown up enough, and I feel a bit trapped, if

I'm honest."

They look at each other, and what comes next surprises the shit out of me.

"You're nearly forty John," Jacob says. "There's no way you're not grown up enough. And she didn't make you quit your job, she asked you. If you really liked it, you'd still be doing it."

I press the button on the lid of my beer, and the heat of my finger tip pops it off. I don't wait for it to cool down, and take a swig straight away. It's Terrell's turn now.

"Ez is a beautiful, beautiful woman John. Why wouldn't you want kids with her? I know what you're like, you're very stubborn. Once you've made up your mind, you stick to it. But this is something you can change your mind about. There are no absolutes here. I think you've said you don't want kids for so long now, that you don't feel you can change your mind without looking like you're going back on yourself, like somehow your pride is at stake. It isn't. You can change your mind. What would you prefer, being back up there, with the twats on that spaceship, or being at home, with a son or a daughter of you own? Being a father," he says putting a hand on my shoulder.

I take another swig of my beer.

"I thought you guys would have been dead against it. What about *the three musketeers?* I think you may be right though. I have been on the fence for a while. I've been arguing with Ez mainly because I didn't want to let go. What do I have to let go of though, really? I'm not young anymore. If I wait too long, and stay on the same page, I'll lose her. And I'll die miserable and alone with nothing and no one." I say.

"And who would we have to pass on our infinite wisdom to? It's not like me or Terrell here are going to have any kids anytime soon. You are the only likely candidate. We'd be like the best uncles ever!" Jacob says with a big grin.

I smile at that.

"The best, or creepiest?" I ask.

"Probably a bit of both. But John, seriously, go for it. What do you have to lose?" Jacob's grin fades a little as he says it.

I didn't have anything to lose. I didn't even know why I was fighting it. So finally, my mind is made up. Jacob and Terrell have completely surprised me. I'm going to get home, and when Ez gets back from work, I'm going tell her we should go for it. And apologise for being such a prick.

We down our drinks, Jacob opens the bottle by the headstone. He pours the beer on the grave, kisses the top of the stone and we silently walk out the way we came in.

18

The next morning I wake up and my head and neck are hurting like bastards. The space beside me on the bed is empty. I guess Ez is at work and has left me to sleep in. After last night's mini epiphany, I literally feel like a new man. Except for the headache and the sore neck that makes me feel like an old man, but hopefully they'll be gone soon. I can't wait for Ez to get home so I can tell her. I decide to make it a special occasion, and plan to get her some flowers and chocolates. I'm really beaming. I feel like a missing part of my life has just been put in place. Why have I been denying it for so long? Oh yeah, I'm a fucking idiot that's why.

I get into the shower and wash off last night's exploits. It's warm straight away, there's no boiling, freezing, boiling, freezing followed by swearing that *Sunspot 2's* showers always give me. And for the first time since quitting, I'm really happy that I'm never going back.

I towel off and get dressed, decide to take the scenic route into town, by the river, when I hear the front door open and slam closed. I walk downstairs to find Ez curled up in a ball on the sofa, crying and visibly shaking. I sit down next to her and put my arm around her.

"What's wrong?" I ask.

She looks up at me, her eyes are blood shot, and it looks like she's been crying for a long time.

"He's gone," she manages.

"Who's gone?" I ask.

"Rupert … he … he's disappeared."

"Didn't you mention him yesterday? It's not even been twenty-four hours yet. He probably just decided to not come in and forgot to tell anyone." I wonder why she's so upset, it seems quite trivial, and I start to get paranoid.

"No, John. You don't understand. He's gone. And he's taken the project we were working on with him."

"The project … ?"

"Yes, I can't say any more than that. Please don't ask. He's been acting very strange recently. He didn't seem to want to finish it. And now he's taken it and vanished. I was working on it as well, and *Skylark* think I had something to do with it. They think I helped him John. I've been questioned all morning. My god, I'm being questioned by government agents tomorrow, if they don't believe me I'll be picked up, tortured and then executed as a traitor. I haven't done anything John, I'm not a traitor, I HAVEN'T DONE ANYTHING!" she screams before curling back into a ball, and continues to cry. I try to reassure her, and tell her that everything is okay, but she's having none of it.

"John, *Skylark* are merciless. There're a lot of things I haven't told you, I didn't want to scare you. People I know have been tortured for just having *Skylark* schematics on their personal computers, they were just behind with their work John, that's all. They were tortured and then imprisoned for that. If they think I've helped steal something this big John … ."

I hold her tightly, it's the only thing I can think to do. I think back to yesterday, with all its hope for the future. When she kissed me goodbye last night it was one of the last times I saw her happy. I never see that beautiful smile again.

19

"John, wake up…"

SLAP!

"John, WAKE UP!"

SLAP! SLAP!

"Alright! I'm fucking awake!" The side of my face stings. I cough instead as I breathe in the smokey air. Kerry smiles at me and I sit up. The bridge is bathed in red light, and a layer of smoke is floating halfway up the room. Luckily, I can hear the loud whine of the air scrubbers doing their job. Kerry holds out a hand, I grab it and she pulls me to my feet. I look around and see Mark sitting at his station, holding his head. His white hair looks as pink as Kerry's in this light. There doesn't seem to be too much damage in here as far as I can tell, just a lot of unsecured objects strewn across the deck. I don't know about the rest of the ship. I look out of the viewports. The stars are moving upwards at speed, followed by the sun, followed by more stars, back to the sun again. That's not a view I've ever seen before. I stand back and rub my eyes. I realise that the impact has sent the ship spinning out of control. After standing up for less than a minute, I can feel how badly my back hurts, and how badly my throat hurts from all the smoke. I hurt all over. I look at Kerry and Mark. They look like they've been through the wars too. Mark's bleeding from the forehead, and Kerry has blood underneath her nose, mixed with soot. I smile at them.

"We're not dead. I'm a little bit surprised by that," I say.

Mark takes his hand off of his head, looks at the blood on it, and puts it back.

"I feel dead. And I get the feeling the ship may be dead too."

Kerry rolls her eyes.

"I love your fuckin' optimism, Mark, we haven't even checked any of the systems yet," she says picking up her chair from the deck and sitting down at her console. She flicks a few switches and presses a few buttons, but there's nothing. The monitors are just showing static.

"The pessimistic fucker's right John. We're dead in space."

"What about the hangar?" I ask, realising there's no

way to tell if it's attached or not without physically looking, so I walk back to the viewports. I have to tip toe to look down to where the hangar should be, and it's there. It's in its housing. That's one thing that has gone right. In a fucked up sort of way, at least.

"We have it … it's attached," I say.

Kerry and Mark look out at the vast solar-panelled top of the hangar deck, and let out almost simultaneous sighs of relief. Mark then starts to look puzzled.

"It looks like it's maybe bowing slightly. As if the impact has bent the housing so it's at a different angle to the rest of the ship. If that's the case, we won't be able to get on board through the adjoining airlocks, they'll be at least three or four metres apart," he says.

I look out again, and I realise he may be right, it's definitely bowing downward.

"It looks like you're right again. Bugger. I'll go down to the cargo bay and check it at the airlock. While I'm gone, see if there's anything you guys can think to do up here," I say heading towards the hatch, then pause and turn around to look at them both and point my finger.

"Except fucking, definitely no fucking."

As I get through the hatch and into the habitation level, I can hear a groaning noise coming from the far end. I get off the ladder and walk through the smoke, which is still thick here, and glowing red due to the emergency lighting. I can't see more than about three metres ahead of me. I notice the air scrubbers don't seem to be on. In my quarters I grab a towel from the deck where I left it earlier and hold it over my face. I hear the groaning again. I realise it's Robert. The panel with the controls for the scrubbers is next to the sick bay door, so I put one hand on the wall and walk to the end as fast as I can. My eyes are streaming by the time I get there, and I can barely see a thing. I can't imagine how Robert's feeling, I'm surprised he's not dead from the smoke inhalation.

I get to the panel and hit the red button. The scrubbers whine into life. I get down to my knees and crawl in through the door, trying to breathe as little as possible. The sick bay is a mess, all the equipment is on the deck, and a lot of it looks smashed. All the beds are on their sides. I can just see Robert underneath one of them. The beds are massive, heavy-duty things. If one were to fall on you, it would very likely break bones. Robert has had a very bad time of it so far today, far worse than me, Kerry or Mark, and a lot of that is down to my actions. His day has probably not as bad as Tim's though, as it's very likely that he's pretty fucking dead.

I crawl over to him. He's making some horrible noises. There's soot under his nose, staining his blond moustache. I shake him slightly, but he doesn't respond. The first thing to do is to get the bed off of him. It's laying on its side pinning down both of his legs. I can see that the air is starting to clear a bit, and

I try and take a breath. I cough, and splutter. Robert wakes up. He starts screaming, doesn't seem to know where he is. I quickly grab the frame of the bed and just about manage to move it. I'm straining with the effort. Just before I get it past his feet, it slips from my grip, and I drop it on his ankles. He screams again but this time he seems to know what's going on.

"You fucking cunt!" he shouts.

I pick it up again and get it off him completely. He's wheezing badly, so I grab a mask off of the wall rack and connect it to one of the oxygen mix tanks, and then attach the mask to his bald tattooed head. His beard makes for a bad seal, but I guess it's better than nothing.

I wait with him for about five minutes and his breathing starts to level off. I stand up and go to the intercom, to get Kerry or Mark down here, but there's nothing but static.

"Robert, stay here and breathe slowly. I'll get Kerry to come down and help you." He nods, and I leave the room. As I walk back to the hatches, I can see smoke rising from down below, which makes me think the engine room must have been on fire. Or still is. And then it occurs to me that we really should have closed all the hatches when we knew we were heading for a collision. Each level has its own life support, and we wouldn't be completely smoked out like we are now. If there had been any sort of massive decompression after the collision, we'd all be dead now. We learned all of this and more in our emergency situation training. The guy taking the course said if you didn't remember everything, it was fine. Because if you do get into an emergency situation out in space, the adrenaline will kick in, and it will all come flooding back. Absolute bollocks. I haven't remembered a fucking thing, and it seems like no one else has either.

20

Once I get back up to the bridge I see that Kerry and Mark are both busy underneath their consoles checking the scorched wiring.

"Kerry ... ?" I say. She looks around, and sits up.

"We're pretty knackered up here John, almost all the fuses are blown and most of the wiring is burned to a fucking crisp."

Mark gets out of from underneath his console.

"Navigation is the same. Burned to a fucking crisp. There is good news though." Kerry and I look at him, hopeful.

"We're spinning out of control and heading straight towards the sun." He forces a smile and then drops his head and closes his eyes. I get the feeling he's beginning to crack.

"Robert's in a bad way in sick bay, and it looks like the engine room is on fire. Kerry, can you keep an eye on Robert and make sure he's okay, while Mark and I tackle the fire and hopefully find Tim alive?"

"Mark's got more first aid training than me, and he's better at it, so I'm coming with you," she says bluntly.

Mark looks up slowly and nods his head in agreement.

Before we get to the engine room, Kerry goes in to her quarters. She comes out with a wet towel, and ties around her head. I do the same with the towel I already have and we head back to the hatch.

"Kerry, do you know where the extinguishers are in the engine room?" My voice is now muffled by the towel.

"I think there are three of the fuckers along the same wall as the hatch, so we climb down, grab them and hope it's not a raging inferno. If that's the case, we close the hatch and open the airlock and let the vacuum of space deal with it."

"Could we not do that now?" I ask.

"Really, John? This was your idea, you remember?! *Tim*! Tim May still be alive, he's got no chance if we blow him into space."

"Oh shit, yeah, sorry. I'm scared and think my brain has stopped functioning."

She nods her head.

"Me, too. Fucking scared. This time though, there's

no pussying out of it, you're going down first."

I make sure the wet towel is tight around my head and then slowly start the smoky descent. I look over my shoulder as we climb down past the rec deck. I can't see all the way to the far end because of the smoke, but I can just about see that all the tables are on their sides, and pool balls are scattered across the deck. We pass through the deck and into the thick smoke of the engine room.

I jump down the last three rungs and quickly grab an extinguisher. Kerry grabs one too and we both turn around to see the damage. Flames are violently spurting out of the open vents on the engine shaft like flame throwers. The fire is burning its way to the fuel tanks, and once it gets there that'll be the end of that.

"John, when I shut off the engines before the crash the fuel tanks were automatically cut off. I'm guessing due to the shit upkeep of the engine shaft, the fuel didn't drain out as it's supposed to. This ship was always a fucking disaster waiting to happen," she shouts through the damp towel. I nod and pull the pin out of the extinguisher and aim at it the closest eruption of flame to me. The foam shoots out. Kerry moves forward and does the same.

Every time it looks like I'm getting the best of the patch of the fire I'm working on, it comes back seemingly even worse. We're running out of time. The fire is making its way closer and closer to the fuel tanks. It's simply too powerful for the extinguishers to deal with, and we're both nearly out of foam. The only option left is to space it. I look at Kerry and point to the hatch, she nods, drops her extinguisher, heads to the ladder and starts up it. I run over and grab one of the rungs, start to climb up behind her, and then stop. Kerry is now in the rec deck, I can see her head through the hatch and she's beckoning me up. I shake my head and drop back to the deck and run for the inspection tubes, realising once again that I've forgotten about Tim. I hear her shout *"No, John!"* as I run across the engine room. I get to the ladder for the gangway and start to climb it. Fucking hell, it's hot; I can barely hold on. Once up I climb the steps to the top inspection tube, turn around quickly and look across the engine room. Flames are everywhere now, closing in rapidly on me and the fuel tanks. I really haven't got any time left. I turn around and open the hatch to the top inspection tube. It opens with a hiss. I look inside. There's about two metres of tube, and then it's crushed flat. As I stare into it a horrible guilt fills me. This is my fault. If I hadn't been so stupid as to drop a spanner into an especially sensitive area, none of this would have happened. How can something so small and insignificant have caused this awful situation? Tim has been crushed doing his best to save us, and he's dead because of my mistake.

He's the first person I've lost under my charge. The thought never even occurred to me that it was a possibility. Everything is so routine, so dull, that nothing bad could ever happen. I know now how out of my depth I am, I know that if I stay in charge, everyone will end up dead because of my idiotic decisions.

I sit down on the gangway facing the tube's hatch and realise I don't want any more of this. I can feel the intense heat of the fire on my back and want nothing more than for it to take me. I close my eyes momentarily. A hard slap to the side of my face snaps me out of it. Kerry pulls me to my feet and pushes me down the gangway stairs. She has a surprising amount of strength in that tiny frame of hers. I stumble but keep my balance. She then jumps over the safety rail and lands on her feet on the deck. I do the same, but land somewhat less gracefully and she pulls me towards the ladder to the rec deck. At the ladder she turns and shouts.

"What the fuck are you doing? We've got almost no time until the fuel tanks blow, and you start feeling sorry for yourself?" She slaps me again, really hard this time, so hard that the towel doesn't take away the sting.

"Now get the fuck up to the rec deck and open the engine room airlock!"

We climb, and behind and underneath us the inferno is raging. Something explodes, and a wave of searing heat hits us. It forces us to move up the ladder faster.

Once in the rec deck, flames start licking through

the hatch as we slam it down behind us. I stand up and run to the panel and enter my codes, and then press the button to open the engine room airlock. We hear a loud whooshing noise below us as the air gets sucked out along with the fire. I take a look out of the rectangular viewport. I can just about see the fire shooting out of the airlock in a short spiral motion because the ship is still spinning. When there's no more oxygen left to fuel it, it fades out around twenty metres from the hull. A strangely beautiful sight.

Kerry rips the towel off of her face and stares at me with tangible hostility.

"I am not dying out here because some jumped up little shit gets a case of the guilts. How dare you force me to make a fucking choice like that?! You could have blown the fucking ship up if I hadn't have got you." She's shaking with rage.

"You could have just shut the hatch and opened the airlock," I say quietly.

"Fuck you. You know what? I probably would have if it were possible. But you're the only one with the fucking access codes."

"My god ... I'm so sorry ... I ... I'm not cut out for this. Every decision I have made has been wrong. Everything I've done so far has fucked us up even more. I don't know what to do anymore ... I ... I ..." I lean against the wall and slide down, and put my hands over my face. Everything from the last twelve hours to the situation with Ez decides to try and escape from me, but I just about manage to hold it together. Kerry sits down next to me, and puts her arm around my shoulders. She waits until I've calmed down, then she whispers into my ear.

"We're still not out of the woods yet, John. You still need to take charge."

I wipe my face with the now black towel.

"You'd do a better job. Everyone at least respects you."

"That may be true, but I fly the ship. You, and only you are going to lead us out of this, whether you like it or not."

I liked it not.

"Did you know I'm not supposed to be here? That I quit at the beginning of our last three month break?" I say.

"No, I didn't," she replies.

"I did. And that makes being here now a massive kick in the balls. I wasn't coming back, that was it. But here I am."

She looks at me quizzically.

"Then why the fuck *are* you here?" she asks.

I wait for a few seconds before I reply, not really knowing how to explain it. Finally, I cop out.

"I'm not really ready to talk about that yet. Maybe when we're out of this mess. Maybe."

I stand up awkwardly and walk towards the cargo bay. The air scrubbers are finally doing their job now that the engine room is sealed off, and I can see clearly. It's a mess. The emergency lighting is still on, so everything has a red hue. I look out of the small round window of the hangar deck airlock, and can see that the hangar is back in place. Unfortunately, Mark was very right, and while it's technically in its housing, the impact has bent the housing downward, there's a gap of about five or six metres between doors, and no seal. Fuck. I'm going to have to get everyone together to come up with some ideas to get around this. With the ship spinning out of control and heading directly for the sun, the desperate need to get on board the hanger deck to find out what has happened to the other half of the crew, and the question of who sabotaged us, we really need to try and work together, and put our differences behind us.

I head back into the rec deck and Kerry is still sitting next to the hatch, just rubbing her face and looking a little beaten. I check the engine room control panel, and see that all the air and fire have now been completely sucked into space. I close the airlock and start the re-pressurisation procedure. I walk over to Kerry.

"What's the plan then John?" she asks.

"To bash our collective broken heads together and get out of this alive. Even though a few minutes ago that's not exactly what I wanted."

She looks at me and rolls her eyes.

"Let's head to the sick bay then," she says, grabbing my hand and pulling herself up.

Mark has Robert sitting on a chair. He's awake and seems in good spirits until he sees me. I hold my hands up in front of me and apologise again. Kerry nods at him and he seems to relax. Fuck knows what that's all about. Whether he's in a piss with her or not, she still has some power over him. And that's to my advantage at the moment.

"You two are a mess," he says. "Where the hell have you been?"

"Heroically putting out raging fuckin' infernos in the engine room. Nothing too exciting," Kerry replies.

Mark stares at us for a few seconds.

"Tim?" he asks.

I look down and shake my head.

"No."

I can feel the guilt flowing from everyone, they all suspected him of sabotage, and he then died saving our lives. I feel the guilt too, but not quite for the same reason.

21

I walk in circles around the small sick bay. I'm thinking that somehow it's up to me to bring everyone together with a rousing and uplifting speech, something that makes us want to get off of our arses and sort out this horrible situation we've found ourselves in. But I can't think of anything rousing or uplifting. I decide to just open my mouth and see what comes out.

"Today has started pretty fucking badly, and has got progressively worse as it has worn on, to the point that we are now spinning towards the sun without any way of stopping ourselves. After the collision and the fire, I seriously doubt the engines will be an easy fix, and the navigation systems on the bridge are all fried."

I've failed to be rousing or uplifting on every level.

"And the communications," Mark adds, lowering

his head.

"And the communications ... fuck. Has anyone got any ideas?" I ask.

Dead silence.

"We need to get into the hangar deck, and the only way to do that at the moment is a space walk to its forward airlock. And I'll be fucked if I'm going out there while we're spinning the way we are, and so close to the sun," I say.

Robert looks up, and I can almost see a light bulb go ping above his head.

"The hangar ... it's got thrusters that are on a separate system to the main engines. That's how to stop us spinning," he says.

"It's a good idea, but that means someone still has to do a space walk. It would be suicide. The way the ship is moving, it'd be too easy to be knocked off into space. And on top of that, anyone going outside would be burned to a crisp in seconds," I say.

"Actually, John, that's not entirely true." Kerry says.

I look at her, confused. She smiles at me, then continues.

"It's freezing out there. There's nothing to conduct the heat. Just vacuum. All you have to worry about is the radiation, and the suits are built to deal with that. To a degree anyway."

"Then why the fuck is this ship completely covered in heat shields then?" I ask, looking around, hoping someone is with me.

Robert smiles.

"It's in case we get hit by a solar flare, or caught in the sun's corona. To be honest though, if that happened, all the heat shields in the universe couldn't save us. You really didn't know that? Really?" he says.

Once again, with my complete lack of knowledge I've successfully made myself look like an idiot.

"I really didn't. Fuck."

I'm now expecting Robert to tear me to pieces, but to my complete surprise, he doesn't. Instead he stands up and limps out of the room holding his left side. When he gets to the door he turns.

"I'm gonna see what you've done to my engine room, before you make up your mind if this suicide mission's an option or not."

With that he's gone. Mark then smiles a scary wide eyed smile.

"Are we going to draw straws for the privilege of killing ourselves then? I'll tell you this now, I'm not doing it. There's no way. I'm not convinced that any one of you isn't the saboteur, and I won't risk my life to find that out. We've eliminated one person, his death trying to save us all makes him a hero in my book. Only three more to go... ."

Kerry gives Mark an angry look, which usually would stop him in his tracks. But this time he doesn't seem to want to stop.

"Not this time Kerry, I don't even trust that you're

not the one who's done this to us. Everyone likes you, and you know how everything works. *You* are in a perfect position to sabotage the ship. Hell, you even knew what was wrong with the engines." He stops, eyes wide and points at her.

"You're the fucking saboteur! I can't believe I didn't see it before, and you've been using sex to keep me on your side all this time … I can't believe that I slept with you and didn't realise! My god, the thought makes me feel sick, as soon as this is over I'm going to … ." She punches him full force in the face and he goes down hard on the deck. She looks at me, her face is a shade of red that clashes with her pink hair.

"It looks like it's just us going outside for a little suicidal space walk then doesn't it?" she says with her face a little too close to mine. I'm not in a position to argue, she's been close to the brink because of me already. One word and I'd imagine she'd kill everyone in sight.

We head back down to the engine room and leave Mark on the sick bay deck plates, unconscious. The place is a blackened mess. Smoke is lazily rising from the uneven looking engine shaft. Robert is standing there staring at the sheer amount of damage and laughing to himself. He holds his ribs, then laughs some more. He sees us and gains a little composure.

"There is nothing I can do. Everything is seized up and warped from the heat of the fire, all the dials, wiring, computers and monitors have melted. Sorry guys. It's properly wankered. It would take months in space dock to fix and they'd probably have to replace the whole engine room. I'm really sorry, but there's only one option left."

"Figured as much," Kerry says. "John, I think we better suit up then."

Fucking hell fucking hell fucking hell.

"I've never done a space walk in my life," I say.

"But you must have done the zero gravity simulator in your basic training, right?"

"No. My training was rushed. I only got a few days. I get the feeling they missed out a lot of the important stuff."

"You're telling me. Fucking hell John, Is there anything you can actually do on this ship?"

"… No, not really, no," I say, lowering my head. Kerry just stares at me for a few seconds, and then looks me up and down.

"Well, at least you're honest."

22

We head back up to the rec deck, and open up one of the storage lockers in the cargo bay. Kerry passes me an old white space suit, which looks pink in the emergency lighting.

"Looks about your size John, get in and I'll zip you up."

I put the suit on apprehensively and she tightens, straps and zips everything up for me. Robert limps into the cargo bay and does the same for Kerry. He then moves to the next locker along and gets out a helmet and starts to attach it to my suit. I hold my breath and the helmet locks into place. The suit is now completely airtight. He turns a valve and the air starts pumping through. I let myself breathe slowly, and notice the air has a horrible metallic taste to it. I feel very claustrophobic with the helmet on, but try and keep myself level headed. When Robert is finished with Kerry, he limps back into the locker and grabs a four metre long tether and clips it to us, and points to the forward most escape pod airlock.

"John, if we're using the airlock without the escape pod, I'm gonna need you to type in the override code." He sounds distant and weirdly compressed through the helmet. I turn and walk past the escape pods and over to the panel and try to type in my code, but the gloves are too thick and I keep hitting two or three keys at once.

"Can't do it, I've got fat fingers with the gloves on. You'll have to."

"What's the code then? Or is it a shift manager secret?" he asks.

I really thought everyone had their own codes. Letting only the shift manager have the codes seems awfully dangerous and stupid to me. What if they went missing?

"It's November, Charlie, Charlie, one, eight, six, four," I say.

He rolls his eyes and types it in and the round airlock door hisses open.

"Once you two are out there, you're on your own. With communications down, there's no way to contact you until you're back. You will be able to talk to each other through the suit's intercom, the on/off switch is on your chest. Honestly though, good luck you guys, hopefully you'll find some good news over there," he says and pats our shoulders.

Kerry looks over to me, I'm feeling tense, and she can see it. She holds out her hand. I grab it without a thought, and we walk to the airlock hand in hand.

"John, you see the glowing little green square on your wrist?" she says through the suits intercom. I nod.

"Well that lets you know how much solar radiation the suit, therefore you, have absorbed. Starts green, and then goes a nice amber."

"So ... amber means dead, right?" I ask.

"Nope. Red means fuckin' dead. Amber only means nearly fuckin' dead."

"Right. Thanks for clearing that up. How long before we're dead then?"

"No idea this close to the sun. For all I know it'll go red straight away. It should be fine though, there are jet injectors in the hangar's control room with some sort of fancy anti-radiation medicine that should stabilise us if we absorb an amber amount," she says and smiles.

"Very reassuring. Have you ever done this? I mean walked on the hull of the ship before?"

"Once, about five years ago, it's a fuckin' doodle. There's a handrail along the side that goes all the way up to the front of the ship, well, hangar, and then you climb a ladder onto the top, and then you're at the other airlock. No big deal."

I let out a small sigh of relief. That didn't sound all that bad. At least there'll be something to hold on to the whole way.

I hear the door shut behind us and tense up again. Suddenly a loud hissing noise fills the little room and I find myself leaving the deck as the artificial gravity dissipates. My feet start moving upward, and my head starts moving backwards, I squeeze Kerry's hand tightly in panic, and she manages to stop me from turning upside down. The outer doors then slowly open, and for the first time ever, I get to see the stars and cosmos with my own eyes. Or at least as close as it's possible to without exploding. For a split second, I'm in complete awe at the majesty of it. But the stars are spinning in a circular motion anti-clockwise, round and round, and the motion starts to turn my stomach. The awe quickly turns to nausea, and the feeling is ruined. The last thing I want is little chunks of sick floating around in my helmet, so I look down at the deck and hope the feeling goes away.

"Okay, John. Follow me." Kerry's voice inside my helmet makes me jump, I didn't notice that it had become so silent.

She lets go of my hand, grabs the right side hand rail and moves herself towards the outer door. She puts her left arm outside the ship, moves it upward, then swings herself out. I float there, helpless and unable to move. I try to reach the rail, but have no way of propelling myself forward. The tether between us gets tighter and I get pulled out towards the spinning stars. Once out of the door I try and grab the handrail above it but miss and start floating away from the ship.

"I've missed the handrail Kerry! Shit, hold on tight or I'll pull you off too," I say.

"No worries, John, I won't let go."

The tether gets to its full length, and with a hard jolt that feels like it may rip through my space suit I stop dead. I just float there for a few seconds. I then slowly start to pull myself in. I unwisely venture a look at the hull. Oh, fucking hell. Kerry is next to a four or five metre gap between the main hull and the hangar, caused by the crash and the bent housing. I hope Kerry has a plan to cross it. I then look down the rest of the hangar and visually try to follow the line of the handrail to the front of the ship. It goes on for about around ten to fifteen metres before it gets cut off by the first of hundreds of different shaped solar panels that cover the entire ship.

"Kerry ... when you did this before, was it before or after the solar panels started getting installed?"

"Why's that?" she asks and looks down the hull. "Oh my fucking god ... I'd say before, then."

This wasn't going to be a doodle. It was now a seventy metre weightless assault course full of jagged pieces of metal, no hand holds on a ship that is trying its best to spin us off of it.

"Any bright ideas?" I ask.

"Only this one: hold on tightly."

She pushes herself off of the handrail and heads

across the gap towards the rail on the hangar, but she judges it wrong and she starts moving upwards and above me as the ship spins. The tether jolts her as it reaches its limit.

"Oh, fuck it," she mutters. She ends up behind me and grabs the rail.

"Your turn," she grins. "When you push off, aim below the rail."

I look at her, then look across the gap, and just push myself off and do what she says and aim low. If I'd stopped to think about what I was doing I would have frozen up. I float past the gap and the rail is ahead but above me. The angle feels right and I'm pretty sure I'll be able to grab it with no trouble. The tether starts to feel like it's tightening, and for a second I think that maybe it's not long enough, but it loosens and I grab the rail with ease.

"John, hold on tight," Kerry shouts, and I look back towards her. She's off the hull and floating out into space. I hold on tightly as the tether once again reaches its limit and she pulls herself in.

"That was a bit scary," she says.

"Did you let go before I'd grabbed the rail?" I ask.

"Had to, I realised the tether wasn't long enough. You looked like you were going to make it, but not if the tether pulled you back, so I pushed out too."

"Fucking hell, that was risky. I'm glad you didn't say anything." I look down the hull, and then back at Kerry. "I guess we should proceed?" I say.

We move forward down the port side of the ship until we get to the first solar panel. It's about half a metre off the hull on metal legs that fortunately for us are on its edges, so they're easy to use as hand holds and we make quick work of it. The next one isn't going to be so easy. It's flat against the hull, and whatever company decided to put it there decided to cut the handrail to put it in place. There's no obvious way to cross it. It's about ten metre square, and a lot longer than the tether. I look up, and see that the panel above us is raised, but I can't see above that as the port side of the hull then banks off at a forty five degree angle for about fifteen metres before it flattens out for the top.

"I think the only way is up, there's no way we're crossing that panel." I say.

Kerry looks along the hull, then up.

"There's not really any other option then, is there?" she replies.

I'm holding onto the edge of the panel we've just crossed. Kerry pushes herself up and grabs hold of the panel above. When it looks like she's got a firm grip, I do the same, leap-frogging over her and grabbing hold of the far edge of the panel. She pulls herself to my position and we can see over the edge.

All the panels on the forty-five seem to be raised, and it looks like there are plenty of hand holds. But that's only for the fifteen metres before it banks again.

We continue to leap frog each other, grabbing

anything to hold us steady, and slowly make our way to the next edge. Once we get there, we look onto the vastness that is the top of the hangar. I see it from the bridge pretty much every day, but had never considered that one day I'd be space walking on it. It looks like more of the same, solar panels of all different shapes, sizes and heights, seemingly put there at random. We should be able to cross it without too much difficulty, I reckon, if we continue doing what we've been doing.

"John, can you have a look at your radiation monitor for me?" Kerry asks, so I look at my left wrist.

"Yeah, it's a sort of a green brown at the moment, I guess that means it's moving into amber. We're about quarter of the way there, so I think that seems about right, probably."

"Mine's bright orange," she says. A cold chill goes through my body. "There's no way I'm going to make it."

"Maybe the light's not working properly?"

"No John. It's working fine," she says far too calmly.

"But we're wearing the same sort of suit, how can the exposure be different?" I ask.

"I put yours on, and Robert put mine on. I should have double-checked everything. I'm not going to make it John, the light is almost red. I'll be dead in minutes. You'll have to go on without me."

I stare at her, eyes wide. I'm trying my best to stop myself breaking down, I'm beginning to well up when a terribly stupid idea pops into my head.

"Follow me." I shout. "I'm not letting you die out here. I'm getting you inside the hangar before that thing turns red. It's time to do something a little bit reckless."

23

I climb on to the first solar panel I come to on the top of the hangar, and work my way around the edge until I'm holding on just in front of it, facing the bow of the ship. Kerry moves beside me.

"Now hold my hand," I tell her. She puts her right hand in my left. "When I say go, use your legs and push off of the edge of the panel as hard as you can."

"Are you fucking mental? The bow of the ship will disappear underneath us as it spins round, and we'll be left floating … ."

She stops and then looks at me with a shocked expression, and I can see she understands what I'm planning. I finish her sentence.

"… Left floating until the ship spins a full one eighty and back to us. By that point we should be far enough ahead to grab on underneath the bow. In theory anyway."

"You're a fucking idiot, this won't work," she says. "But thank you."

I wait until the sun comes up directly ahead of us, and use it as a giant target so we don't shoot off in the wrong direction.

"Go!"

We both push off with as much force as we can, and move forward steadily above the hangar, narrowly missing a solar panel. The hull below us quickly starts moving downward and then out of our view. For about ten seconds it feels like we're the only ones out here, alone in space and hurtling towards the sun at around one hundred and forty thousand kilometres per hour. With nothing small enough ahead to use as a reference point, it feels like we're not moving at all.

Suddenly the bridge and crew area at the stern start to overtake, barely ten metres below us. It spins forward and around and we can see the three huge boosters, now cold and dark, and then the whole underside of the ship.

"When the bow comes back around, try and grab a hold of whatever you can. There are four re-fuelling tubes on the front of the housing, so there should be stuff everywhere to grab on to. Hopefully we'll be okay. If I remember correctly, and I know that doesn't bode well, there should be a load of hand holds either side of the giant space door at the bow that should lead up somewhere close to the airlock. We're also gonna have to turn round or we won't be able to see anything to grab onto," I say.

She squeezes my hand lightly in acknowledgement, and I can see that she's looking very pale. With my left arm I pull her towards me, until we're facing each other.

"Kerry, with your left hand, grab hold of my right hand, and then let go with your right." Sluggishly, she moves her left hand. When I feel it touch mine, I grab hold of it tightly and let go with my left hand. We move apart and are now facing the opposite way, and the underside of the rapidly approaching bow.

"Are you ready?" I ask, but I don't get a reply. I notice that her hand has gone limp, and I'm now the only one holding on. I look down at her radiation monitor and my heart sinks. It's bright red.

There's no time to think about it as the bow gets closer and closer, so I let go of her as it bears down on us. I hold my arms out and try to grab on to something, anything. But I miss everything as it passes by. The hand holds next to the space door are less than a metre away from my grasping hands as they speed past. I can then see the top of the hangar deck again as the last rung passes by out of my reach. I know that was the only chance I had. The next time the ship spins back to this position we'll probably be ten to fifteen metres ahead of it with no hope of getting back on board. Fuck.

Suddenly my tether starts to get tight and the ship doesn't seem to be moving downwards anymore. I look down, and see that by a miracle Kerry has managed to grab hold of one of the last handholds. Thank fuck. I realise that she probably had to use her last bit of strength to do it, so I pull myself towards her as quickly as I can before she lets go. I grab hold, and look at her pale face.

"I knew you'd fuck that up," she whispers, forcing a half smile. She closes her eyes and I know I have no time to lose. I climb up to the edge and onto the top of the hangar. The handholds carry on flat across it up to the airlock's hatch. I look back and see that Kerry has let go and is floating unconscious behind me.

Rung by rung I pull myself towards the hatch knowing that it's too late for her, knowing that there's no way to save her now, but I'm still clinging on to a small sliver of hope that the jet-injectors will save her.

I get to the hatch and pump the handle a few times and then turn the wheel on top of it one-handed. It opens without a sound, and I climb down into the airlock. Once I'm in, I carefully pull Kerry down through the hatch and then close it behind her. I move down to the control panel by the door and type in the code to turn air and the gravity back on. Luckily with this control panel, someone has had the foresight to make the buttons big enough to use with chunky gloves on. I move Kerry down onto the deck plate so when the gravity generator starts up she doesn't drop and smash the glass on her helmet, not that that really matters now, I guess.

There's a quiet humming noise and I start to feel myself slowly move downwards until my feet are back on the deck. We've only been outside for about twenty minutes, but everything feels so much heavier than it did when we set out. I can barely stand up and hold the weight of my spacesuit. I'm expecting the green light to come on, so we can get on board the hangar, but it stays red. I look at the display on the panel, and it says no oxygen is being pumped through. Can anything else go wrong? for fuck's sake. Without the pressure being equalised, the door will never open and we'll be stuck in this tiny shitty airlock. But then, as I'm beginning to think the worst, the light turns green and the door does open. I look at the display again, and it still reads no oxygen. Oh, fuck it. The reason the door has opened is because the pressure was already equalised. There is no air on board the hangar. The crash must have knackered the tanks somehow. This is going to make things much more difficult.

With a lot of effort I manage drag Kerry out of the airlock and on to the upper gangway, I un-tether myself from her and awkwardly try and run to the thruster control room, which is quite difficult in a spacesuit.

Once in, I look around for a first aid box or something that would hold the injectors, but with the flickering emergency lighting it's hard to see anything. There's nothing in here and I turn to leave and look somewhere else when I spot a lit up red box on the same wall as the door. I open it up and tip the contents onto the console and spot what I'm looking for. A smaller rectangular box that has a radiation symbol with a cross running through it printed on the side. I grab it, and run back to where I left Kerry. My hands are shaking as I open the box and remove one of the jet-injectors, I quickly glance at the instructions printed on the inside and click the safety catch off. I press it to her arm, and notice that she doesn't seem to be breathing anymore. I pull the trigger, and with a quiet hiss it administers the dose. I pray it's powerful enough to get through all the layers of a space suit. I wait a minute or so, and nothing.

Kerry said earlier that you give one dose for an amber amount of radiation, but she said nothing about how much for red (Dead). Maybe there's no point, but I'm not ready to give up yet. I put the injector to her arm and give her another dose, maybe two shots will undo the red exposure, but still nothing. I do it again, and then again and then scream as loud as I can. Out of desperation I start chest compressions, and keep going for what seems like ages until my arms and back ache from the effort. I then look at her pale face through the helmet, and know she's gone. There is nothing left to do. I've failed her. I slump down and lay my head down on her chest. I don't know why I try to hold it back, I guess it's from years of trying to be an emotionally repressed grown up. But with no appearances to keep, with no one left around to be strong for, I let it all out, and I cry harder than I ever have.

24

I lie on the metal gangway next to Kerry, staring at the ceiling through the steamed up glass of my helmet. I know I'm here on a mission, I know I've got to stop the ship spinning out of control, I know I've got to search for Tom and his crew. But I don't have the motivation anymore. The one person on board I would have tried to save is lying next to me, dead. The other two pricks in the crew compartment can go fuck themselves as far as I'm concerned. At this moment, I really don't care if they live or die.

My thoughts start turning to my life before this fucked up situation, and back to Ez, and that fucked up situation. If I get back I'm going to have to try and fix everything with her, and there is a lot to fix. The last three weeks of our time together was awful, she needed help and I was a selfish shit. If it's even possible to save what we had, I have to try my hardest. And that can't happen if I'm stuck on board a spaceship hurtling towards the sun. I know now that I want to survive, I have to. I'm not going to do this to save Robert or Mark, I'm going to do it to save myself. If they get saved in the process, well, I guess that's a bonus for them.

I stand up, pick up the second jet-injector and give myself a shot. I needn't have worried about it not getting through the space suit, because it stings like a bastard. I walk back to the thruster control room and try and work out how to get the thrusters working and aim them. This is what Kerry was supposed to do, she knew how everything worked on this ship. She would have just hit a few buttons, flicked a few switches and it would have been sorted. I'm just going to have to guess.

The big red button next to the thrust velocity lever seems like a good place to start, so I press it. The console lights up and a target looking graphic appears on the monitor. An alarm starts blaring, and a female computer voice tells me we're in imminent danger due to being off course and spinning wildly out of control. Like I didn't know that already. It then asks if I want it to correct our course and trajectory. It can't be that simple can it? I click *yes* cautiously. The whole hangar bay starts to vibrate as the thrusters fire. I look out of the view port above the monitor, and the stars slowly stop moving upwards until only the sun is shining through. Turns out it can be that simple. If Tim were still alive, I think he'd have some explaining to do. The payload specialists are paid to take over from the pilot at the final stages of the drop. To aim the ship precisely so the waste materials get incinerated as efficiently as possible, otherwise they may slingshot around the sun and head back out into the solar system. The waste can then become a massive danger to shipping, and even possibly get back to Earth. A few cruise liners were damaged this way, and the United Governments intervened and made it law to have someone on-board for that specific task. And it turns out a fucking computer does it. The dump specialists must have an excellent union, or someone high up has had a nice kick back.

The vibrations stop as the thrusters switch off.

"Final drop co-ordinates confirmed. Five hours and seven minutes to optimum drop point," the computer tells me. I didn't realise we were so close. So far so good, now I guess I have to search this place for any signs of Tom and his crew. This is the part that has me the most anxious. A big part of me doesn't want to find them. If they are responsible for any of this situation, I don't know what they'd do if I suddenly turn up and say "Hi." And now I don't even have back up. And for that at the very least, Tom has to pay.

I walk out of the thruster control room on to the metal gangway that circles the top level of the hangar deck, move to the safety rail and look down at the hundreds and hundreds of metal containers stacked down there in rows. In the flickering light, I can just about make out that the crash has knocked quite a few of the containers down. In some places it's caused a domino effect. I'm hoping it looks worse up here than it actually is. But I'm definitely going to need a torch. I turn around and go back into the thruster control room, making a point to not look in the direction of the airlock, to where Kerry is lying. I can't think about that. I need to try and keep focused. Quickly scanning the room, I spot a large flashlight attached to the wall next to where the medi-kit was. I grab it and slowly walk aft down the starboard gangway, towards the stairwell that'll take me down to the bottom deck.

Once I get to the rear of the hangar, I peer through the small round window of the airlock that would normally take you into the cargo bay and crew section. We normally leave this door open, and just walk onto the hangar deck if we need to do any final checks, or get to the thruster control room. Now there's a four or five metre gap between the doors, with nothing but vacuum between. For a few seconds I stare into the red light of the crew section, and jump when I see something move. It's Mark. I can only see his head through the window, but he waves at me with his fingers in front of his face. I wave back, and he mouths "I'm sorry." He looks down, and I can tell from his expression that he regrets his recent actions, and most definitely the last thing he said to Kerry.

Fortunately for him though, at this moment he doesn't know that it's the last thing he will ever have said to her. I move away, the thought of his reaction when he finds out makes my heart sink and I'm in danger of my emotions getting the better of me again. The only thing to do is to walk to the edge of the stairwell, and only think about what's happening right now, not dwell on the past or the future. I look down into the murky blackness. It really is dark down there, so I turn on the torch. It flickers a couple of times, so I hit it and comes to life. That doesn't bode well, and I start thinking about monsters again. I start the descent into darkness, one slow step at a time.

The metal containers are about three metres square, usually piled four high, and five or six across depending on load, with enough room to walk between each row. As I reach the bottom deck I shine the torch through the first gap I come to. There is a way through, but the second and third piles are leaning precariously against each other, and I'm not sure I want to risk it collapsing on me. I walk towards the port side of the hangar and shine the torch through the second walkway, but there is no way through. It's like there's been an avalanche of giant cubes. I shine the torch through the third walkway and the light almost reaches all the way to the giant space door at the front of the hangar, and all the containers look close to how they should. That's the way to go then.

I cautiously make my way down the aisle, shining the torch through each gap I come to, making the shadows dance around me. I keep thinking I see something in the corner of my eye, but it must be the light of the torch combined with my imagination. It's horribly eerie down here, the lights on the top deck are flickering, but barely penetrating, and a there's a slow moaning creaking coming from the uneven towers. I move deeper into the maze of containers and begin to realise that I'm not even sure what I'm looking for. Where could five people be hiding down here? There's no oxygen at the moment, so they'd have to be in space suits, or in a container with an air supply. Which is something I've never heard of before.

It's all beginning to seem unlikely that there could be anyone down here at all, or that I'll find anything to figure out what the fuck has been going on when suddenly there is a loud groaning noise. I look around, and see that one of the huge towers is slowly collapsing in my direction. With a loud bang it's halted by the tower in front of it. I sigh with relief, and I'm about to continue my search when the loud metallic groaning starts again. I turn around and both towers are now moving. Together they hit the next one along and that barely halts the momentum. I turn and run as the towers of giant cubes start a domino effect all around me. I can't run at any speed in this space suit, and the collapsing cubes start to overtake me so I stop and hold my arms in front of my helmet and close my eyes.

Almost as suddenly as it started, the groaning and clanking stops. I open my eyes, and have a look around. I shine the torch at the collapsed cubes, and at the path in front of me. The towers just kept collapsing forward until there were no more towers to collapse against, and just stopped. Not a single cube fell in my path. I let out a massive sigh of relief. I almost start to think that I was lucky, and then I remember why I'm down here. Luck can do one.

I stay where I am for a minute or so, shining the torch around, and making sure that everything that's going to fall down has done so, at least for the moment, when the light of my torch catches a container with its door slightly ajar. No container should have an open door. The risk of contamination is too great. Every one of them is welded shut before they are loaded on board because of the awful things that are inside, and the design of the things makes them almost indestructible so they don't leak or crack until they hit the sun's corona and burn up. But here I am, shining a light on one that doesn't even seem to have been welded shut in the first place. I clearly know nothing.

I'm going to have to look inside. I don't want to. Nothing good can come of this, but what other choice do I have? I hold the torch with my left hand and slowly pull the door open wide enough for me to fit through. It squeals loudly, as if it doesn't want me to open it, as if it's protesting at my intrusion. I shine the torch in, and it seems that the only thing in here is a two metre long rectangular wooden crate. Very strange. I walk through the door keeping the torch fixed on the crate as I close in on it, my hand is shaking slightly causing the shadow the torch is creating behind the crate to jitter around. There doesn't seem to be anything out of the ordinary about it, it just seems to be a standard shipping crate. What is out of the ordinary is that it's here, in a container that should be sealed shut. I notice that there was something written along one of the wooden slats that has been badly scraped off. I can make out a few of the letters but nothing more. *S*, *L*, and think an *R*. It means nothing to me so I shine the torch around it a bit more. The lid is nailed shut, but it's not on straight so I'm guessing it's been taken off and banged back on recently.

I start to look on the floor for a hammer or something when I notice a small pool of something dark just at the bottom of the crate. My heart starts beating faster, it can't be what I think it is. I lean down for a closer look, and it's dark red. Oh fuck, I think it's blood. I stand up straight, and begin to slowly move around the outside of the crate. I shine the torch on the deck behind it and jump as I see a body lying there in a pool of blood. I'm not sure what else I really expected to see, but I was really hoping it would be something else, or nothing at all. I close in on it, and realise with horror that it's Tom, and I think his throat has been slit. I don't know how I manage to do it, but I get closer and have a look at the neck wound. His throat has been ripped wide open, and the cut is so deep, I can actually see part of his spine. Nausea hits me. I instantly vomit in my helmet, and have to look away. Luckily, only the bottom part of the helmet's glass gets splattered so I don't have an issue seeing, unless I look straight down. I stand still for a while in shock. It's only when I start to feel the sick begin to trickle down my neck and chest that I decide it's time to move away.

I'm not sure why I do it, probably morbid curiosity, but I venture one more look at the corpse, and something just underneath the throat gash glistens in the torch light. Oh my fucking god, it looks like the same translucent slime I saw in the inspection tubes, and in the cargo bay. I slowly walk backwards out of there, keeping the torch on the body until I'm around the corner of the crate. My heart is beating fast, and I can't collect my thoughts. My mind is racing. Then, I feel something touch my shoulder.

25

Screaming, I drop the torch. It bangs against the deck and instantly goes out. I'm a dead man. I drop to my hands and knees and crawl into the darkness of the container. I sit still against the wall trying to keep my breathing slow and steady, hoping that whatever that was won't be able to find me. I can hear a shuffling as whatever it is moves around, and then there are a couple of banging noises and the torch flickers back into life and shines directly at me. All I can see is the light, and I put my hand in front of my eyes. With uneven footsteps it gets closer and closer, and when the torch is only a few centimetres from my face it stops. What can I do? I'm completely fucked. I've tried my best. And my best was fucking useless. I hold both my arms out and give up, there doesn't seem to be any point carrying on now. The light then moves away from my face and onto the face of whatever this thing is. All I can see is a big purple blob, where the torchlight has blinded me. It slowly fades and I can begin to make out what's looking at me. It takes a few seconds to click, with the light shining underneath the pale face it looks like a creature from an old horror film, but I start recognising the features and I finally see that it's Kerry. It's fucking Kerry! I have never been so relived. Or so completely confused. She tries to say something, but I can't hear anything. I look down at her chest, and point to her radio. She looks down and presses the button.

"Who turned my fucking radio off?" she says in a quiet hoarse voice.

"I guess I did by mistake when I did chest compressions on you."

"You did chest compressions? Oh … well I think you've broken a few of my ribs then you prick," she says then smiles. "Thank you for saving me."

"I thought you were dead. After four hits with the jet-injector and a whole fuck load of chest compressions, you still weren't moving. I really thought you were gone."

"Four hits? fucking hell! I must have looked pretty fuckin' dead. Did you check if I was breathing or had a pulse?"

"No, there was no way to tell, I couldn't take your suit off because there's no oxygen in here anymore. You just weren't moving. You really did look dead. I am very very glad you're not though," I say and give her a big awkward space suit hug.

"You've got sick in your helmet," she says.

"I know, it stinks. Have a look over there," I nod towards the crate.

She pulls away and shines the torch at it, and down to the small pool of blood coming from underneath it. She pulls a face then walks round to the back of the crate. I hear her gasp.

"John, oh my sweet Jesus. What the fuck has happened? Tom's almost had his head ripped off."

Reluctantly I walk back around to the body.

"Look," I say and grab her hand and point the torch at the translucent slime underneath the wound.

"What is it?"

"I'm not sure, but I've found the same substance in the inspection tubes and in the cargo bay where I thought the hangar release control panel used to be." She looks horrified.

"But you never mentioned it," she says.

"I know. I thought I'd be laughed off the ship if I tried to suggest there was some sort of creature on board causing this, so I kept quiet."

"I guess that's fair enough. That would have definitely happened. We'd have made you look like a proper dick. But, fucking hell. Something on board is killing us off? That sounds a little bit too fucking sci-fi for me. But at the same time, it's the only thing I can wrap my head around, or that makes any fucking sense," she says.

"We've got to get back to the crew section, let Robert and Mark know, and beat our collective heads together and find a way to catch and kill this slime-dribbling bastard before it takes anyone else down," I say.

"But John, where's the rest of Tom's crew? Are we going to find them all down here with their throats ripped open? And what do you think is in that wooden crate?" Kerry points at it.

"No idea. I'm not sure I want to know. If it's got anything to do with this monster, it can't be good."

"We're going to have to try and open the fucker up. Hold this for me." She passes me the torch and goes up to the crate. I shine it at her as she tries to prize off the lid with her gloved hands to no avail.

"Your turn," she says walking back to where I'm standing and grabbing the torch off me.

"I'll give it a go, but I can't see myself shifting it, I'm really very weak," I say and put my fingers under the edge of the lid. Where it hadn't been put back on straight there is a good amount to grip on to. I hold my arms straight and lift with my knees putting in as much effort in as I can. Whatever is in the crate must be ridiculously heavy as it doesn't move at all, but I feel a slight cracking in the lid.

"Kerry, can you grab the other side, I think I'm getting somewhere here."

She puts the torch on the floor of the container with the light facing us and grabs the other side of the lid.

"When I count three, we lift okay?" She nods. "One ... Two ... Three."

We lift simultaneously, still the crate doesn't move, but with a loud cracking sound the lid snaps off. Without thinking, I throw it over the back and it lands with a squelch. Kerry looks at me and shakes her head. For a few seconds I feel absolutely awful.

"I won't tell anyone if you don't," she whispers, and turns around and picks up the torch. She shines it into the box, and I can't make head or tail of what's in there. Tubes, wires, and pipes surrounding something cylindrical. Everything looks like it's all been put together at random then housed in a rectangular metal framework.

"What is it?" Kerry asks.

"I really don't know. It looks like it's some sort of pump, maybe?"

Kerry shines the torch around it some more.

"Maybe. But it's not like anything I've ever seen before." Suddenly there's a loud creaking noise just outside of the container, and we both look at each other.

"I don't like the sound of that," I say.

Kerry heads for the door and looks outside.

"John, what if the thing you're talking about is in the hangar with us?" she says. I look inside the crate one more time, then back to Kerry.

"Then we have to leave, and right now," I say.

"No argument from me, let's get the fuck out of here."

With that we exit the horror cube and run through the maze of waste containers until we get back to the stairwell that heads up to the gangway at the very top. We're both out of breath when we get there, but I notice that Kerry is a lot more than me.

"I'm not running anymore John, I was dead a few minutes ago, I don't want your efforts to be in vain. To die of a heart attack by running up those fucking stairs, well, it would be a massive a kick in the cunt."

So we walk up them, but I keep looking behind us. I offer my hand and she just looks at me and keeps going. At the top, she looks through the knackered airlock window and into the cargo bay.

"The light in there was red earlier, I guess Robert has sorted out the emergency lighting," she says absently, and continues to walk. We make our way quickly down the starboard gangway, towards the thruster control room and the forward airlock.

"How are we going to get back?" I ask her. "I think I've sorted it so the ship is now on its usual course and not spinning out of control. That should make getting across the hangar easier, but what about the radiation?"

"As long as we're quick we should be okay. My radiation monitor is back on green. We'll be fine. But I'm not coming back here again once we've left. I want whatever that thing is, and whatever is in that crate off the ship." She then walks into the thruster control room and starts pressing buttons.

"What are you doing?" I ask.

"I'm setting it to dump the containers when we get to the co-ordinates, and then to automatically head back for home once it's done it. We won't have to come back to the hangar again, it's all programmed in. It'll take a lot longer getting home with just these thrusters, but we should get picked up before that."

"And you managed to say all of that without swearing," I say and grin. She looks a little confused.

"What … ? Oh, fuck you."

"Better," I say. She sighs and heads for the airlock, picks up the tether that's lying on the deck and attaches it to herself. She moves over and clips the other end to me.

"After hitting me with four doses of that anti-radiation shit, I don't think my body will be able to cope with any more. So when I say we have to be quick this time, I mean it."

"The roof of the hangar looked easier going than the side did. I think we should go that way until we get to the crew section and then work our way down," I say.

"Okay then. Let's be on our merry fuckin' way."

I hit a few keys on the airlock control panel, and we start to rise as the gravity begins to dissipate. Kerry moves upwards, opens the hatch and moves outside. She missed all of this last time, but as usual she knows exactly what she's doing and I follow her quickly, as she's not hanging around. The roof of the hangar is a much easier option than the side, the solar panels are still all over the place but a lot more uniform. It also helps that the ship is no longer spinning. We get across to the crew section in no time by using the same leapfrog technique as before, and to the gap where the hangar is bowing downwards away from it. Without a word Kerry climbs over the edge and down into the gap, and I have no choice but to follow. She spots something to grab onto on the crew section and pushes herself towards it. I push off too, and we're both now holding on to the other side. She edges herself along the small shelf toward the port side edge and then moves round the corner. To my amazement we're on the right level for the escape pod airlocks. She grabs the hand rail and then let's herself in.

Once I get in she closes the door and starts the re-pressurisation and artificial gravity. I look at her radiation monitor and it's still just green. I think we did okay. We touch down on the deck plates and my suit once again starts feeling a lot heavier than it did before.

"How are you feeling?" I ask her.

"A little bit woosy, but I think I'll survive."

The little light above the control panel turns green and the door into the cargo bay automatically opens. Kerry unclips her oxygen, and with a hiss lifts her helmet off.

"Holy fuck it feels like heaven to finally get that thing off."

She does the same for me, and I hope that I don't get splattered by the vomit that came out of me earlier, but it's pretty much congealed now. When my helmet comes off, it's hard to describe how good the air smells after breathing in the contents of my stomach for the last half hour. She gets out of her suit with no effort then helps me out of mine, as I'm struggling somewhat.

"Your work shirt has sick all down it," she says and I look down.

"I'll go change it soon, but where is everyone?" She looks around, and starts toward the door onto the rec deck when suddenly the lights go out. In the pitch black I hear some footsteps, followed by a thud, and then the sound of a body falling to the floor. The footsteps head towards me and before I can do anything there is a flash, followed by a sharp pain on my right temple and my knees buckle and I'm out. Again.

26

"Why are you here drinking with us? Aren't you supposed to be at home making babies?" Jacob says and downs what's left of his litre of lager. He's absolutely right, I should be, but ever since Ez's boss disappeared with what she only calls *the project* she has completely lost the plot and lives in a paranoid haze. All she does is spend her days in the house with the doors locked and the curtains closed drinking bottle after bottle of vodka and getting through opiates like there's a world shortage.

"I know. But I can't talk to her. At the moment, she won't even talk to me. She just stares at me and then breaks down in tears, and then calls me every insult under the sun. I've never seen her like this. The situation has hit her badly."

Jacob clicks his fingers and the waitress comes

over.

"That was rude," she says to him. He smiles. She smiles back. "You want three more then?"

"I do indeed my love. Just keep them coming." She does a mocking bow and walks back to the bar. Terrell looks at Jacob.

"What have you been up to? Last time we were in here she couldn't stand the sight of you," he asks.

"I have my ways." He looks over to the bar and winks. Terrell shakes his head.

"You're disgusting, and I'm completely jealous. John here, however, I'm not jealous of."

"And I don't blame you," I say. "I think she's had a full mental breakdown. I'm thinking it may be in her best interest to be temporarily sectioned."

They both just look at me, and I can tell by the look on their faces that they didn't fully realise it had got this bad. Or maybe they think I'm way overreacting.

"John, are you sure? That does seem a little bit extreme. Just because she's being all paranoid, doesn't mean *Skylark* aren't out to get her. Especially if they think she's helped to steal a weapon or whatever this *project* is supposed to be. Hopefully that's not the case. Haven't you ever read about what bastards they are?" Jacob asks.

"Um, no. I sort of live in a bubble. I didn't mean to live in one, but with all the shit that seems to constantly be going on in the world and the solar system, I just stopped watching the holobox. Only use it now for films and downloaded TV shows."

"That's why you always seem so clueless about current events," Terrell says.

"Look, I know that I may be going over the top. I know nothing about what *Skylark* do. But I am scared that Ez will hurt herself. She is acting mental. Can you guys come back to my place after this? I don't want to go back by myself, and maybe you'll see what I mean. Or not. I think I need some guidance."

"From us? Really?" Jacob says. "You are lost then." Terrell nods his head.

"Okay. We'll go home with you. But you'll have to treat us like proper ladies."

27

We have three more drinks, partly because going home is not a nice idea, and I know that Ez doesn't really like Jacob or Terrell no matter how much she says she does. Once I've finished my last drink, Jacob calls a taxi and we head back to my place. The maglane takes the taxi to the city limits, but once out of them it has to use the road like any normal car. It takes a while, but finally we're outside my house. All the lights are on, but the curtains are closed. We walk up the drive and I can hear a dull thudding coming from the house. Worried and confused, I run through the front door and find that the front room is full of people dancing and milling about. I have no idea what's going on. Suddenly the music stops and Ez runs up to me and gives me a huge hug.

"Happy birthday, John," she says in my ear. Everyone in the room cheers.

"But it's not my ... ." I suddenly realise it definitely is my birthday and the situation with Ez has made me completely forget about it. Ez lets go of me and looks at Jacob. He holds his hands up in the air.

"Look John, we were supposed to guide you back home earlier than usual, but when you suggested it yourself we didn't have to." Oh fuck. I brought them here to validate what I'd been saying about Ez all night, and it turns out that Ez has been in contact with them anyway. If anything, it now looks like I should be the one who's sectioned. I feel sort of betrayed, and start to wonder if this has all been in my head.

Once the music starts up again Jacob grabs me and pulls me to one side.

"John, I know what you're thinking, but this was arranged weeks ago. We've had no contact with Ez since *Jupiter rising*. We just followed the plan set out for us, and hoped that after what you said this evening, it was still going ahead. We expected Ez to contact us again, but she didn't. It was probably as much a surprise for her as for you that guests started turning up. I believe you. You have your quirks and issues, but this is the first time I've ever seen you this scared and worried," he says.

"Yeah, I am. Even more so now," I reply.

The party seems to go on without incident, and I just stand in the kitchen with Jacob and Terrell. I notice that most of the people here are either Ez's friends or older friends that for one reason or another have drifted away to have families or found newer and more exciting friends. One by one as the night rolls on they come up to me and try and start conversation, but I'm just not interested, my head is elsewhere. So I give one word answers and try to make the conversations as awkward as possible until they go away.

By about midnight most people have gone, none bothering to say goodnight to me. When Terrell and Jacob finally leave at about one it's only Ez and me left.

"Are you okay … ?" I ask her, sheepishly.

"I can't believe you were so rude to all your friends John. I put so much time and effort into this. What's gotten into you?"

I stare at her, completely at a loss for what to say. This is the first time she's spoken to me properly in weeks. She then looks down, and sits on the arm of the sofa.

"Look, I'm sorry John. I think the worst is over. I go back to work next week. It seems like *Skylark* finally believe that I had nothing to do with the missing project."

"So you're no longer under investigation?" I ask.

"I don't think so, no."

"Thank fuck, that's excellent news. I'll get us a drink. Hopefully we can put this behind us and move forward."

"Move forward to where?" She raises an eyebrow and I move in to kiss her. Just as our lips touch there is a grating sound from the front window. Thinking it's either Jacob or Terrell I flip the bird in that direction. But then the front window smashes inward, shards of glass fly everywhere and I instinctively throw Ez to the floor and use myself as cover. Everything then goes quiet and I wonder what the fuck has just happened. There is a quiet buzzing noise, and then a small chrome sphere floats into the room. I hold very still as it slowly moves towards us, it then stops dead in mid-air and shines a green light at Ez.

"Oh no, that's a tracker drone," she whispers.

"A what?"

"It's locked on to me, you have to get out of here. It'll follow me until someone comes to turn it off or eliminate whatever it's locked on to," she says.

"How the fuck do you know this?" I ask loudly, and the drone moves closer. I shut up.

"I helped design it," she says matter of factly. "I thought one would turn up earlier, that's why I was so scared. It's like a countdown, but you don't know what the countdown is for. It could just be watching me, it could be a precursor to something a lot more awful. You simply don't know. And because it follows you everywhere, everyone can see that you're being watched. People assume you've done something anti-government and report on you. When they said I could go back to work, I thought it was over."

"They're using something you designed against you? That just plain sucks," I say.

"It's probably just watching me. Making extra sure I'm telling the truth. But now it's actually here, I don't think I feel all that bad about it. I've done nothing wrong, so this will prove it for sure."

I see a reflection on the shiny metal of the drone, and from the corner of my eye I see Jacob sneak into the room. The drone appears not to have noticed him, and he grabs a tea towel from the kitchen side. With one quick movement, he throws it over the drone and twists it underneath so it can't escape. He then proceeds to use the tea towel like you would a sock full of coins, and starts to bash it against the kitchen side again and again. When he's had enough of that, he then bashes it against the floor again and again just to be sure. Ez stares at him with her mouth agape. Jacob opens the towel, and tiny broken bits of technology fall to the floor. Terrell then pokes his head into the room.

"All sorted then?" he asks.

"Yep, I've fucked it," Jacob says with a wide grin. I stand up, walk over and give him a big hug.

"What have you done?" Ez says shakily, with her eyes wide. Jacob's grin turns to confusion.

"Saving the day I thought," he replies.

"You've just ruined everything! Oh my god, you've made me look completely guilty! You've just killed me!" she shouts.

"Fuck off have I! What would you have done if you were walking away from one of your best mate's houses and then hear the window get smashed in? And when you leg it back there, you find out that there's some sort of floating metal bastard in with them looking all fucking sinister, and that said friend and girlfriend are laying on the floor possibly dead? You'd do something. And I fucking did." He looks furious. And he's right. What else could it have looked like?

Ez doesn't say anything, she just picks up the wreckage of the drone and puts it on the kitchen side. She then sits on one of the barstools around the island that joins the kitchen and the lounge. She whispers something that I can't quite hear, but think I know what it was.

"What was that?" I ask.

"Get out." That's what I thought. I walk over to Jacob and Terrell.

"Probably best if you guys go. Thanks for your help, I'll see you tomorrow."

Jacob nods, and Terrell just looks confused, but they head for the door. I turn around to go and comfort Ez, but she's standing right behind me, and I almost bump into her.

"And you," she says.

"What have I done?" I ask.

"What have you done?!" she repeats my question with complete exasperation.

"You brought those cunts in to my life. Everything I've done since we've been together has been completely for us. Everything you've done, it's just been for you and those two. You will never see the bigger picture. And after everything, one of your precious drinking friends may have just ruined or ended my fucking life. My parents hate you. And finally, after all this time I'm beginning to see why. Get out get out get out GET OUT!"

She pushes me out of the front door and slams it behind me. I walk slowly down the driveway. My head is a mess. I'm not even sure what's just happened. After the last few weeks, I thought our relationship was close to being over. I was going to leave. It was selfish of me but I just couldn't take it anymore. I only stayed because a small part of me knew she needed my help, and I couldn't keep that part of me quiet. For a few fleeting seconds this evening I could almost see a light at the end of the tunnel. But it went out, and the tunnel seems darker now than ever. Is she being paranoid? I really thought she was. Now after the drone incident, it seems I was way off the mark. Have Jacob's actions put her in danger? I hope not. But it's hard to know when Ez won't tell me anything except for tiny fragments of information that I simply don't know what to do with. I need to help her, but I just don't know how. Maybe my original plan would still work? Maybe getting her sectioned would keep her out of harm's way. On every level it's a terrible idea. I knew it before, and I still know it. How could I do that to her? She's the woman I'm supposed to be in love with and I'm planning on sending her to a mental hospital. I'm a fucking dick. And everything she said is probably right.

Jacob and Terrell are waiting at the bottom of the driveway under a street lamp. They are both smoking badly rolled cigarettes.

"You know those things are illegal?" I say half-heartedly knowing that they know, and knowing that they know that I know that they know.

"Yeah, but sometimes there's nothing better for a stressful situation," Jacob says.

"Probably best that I have one then, I've just been kicked out, and Ez thinks that you've killed her."

"They're annoyingly addictive, so I'm probably just gonna give you a joint instead. Unless you want an *Emergency Stop?* Got a couple in my man bag," Jacob says.

"No, actually I don't think I will. But I could do with a place to stay for a few days while I work out what to do."

"Shall we go and see my mother? That's always a good head clearer."

We once again head to the cemetery in the dead of night, and all sit down on the rickety bench that Jacob and Terrell made in complete silence. The sun is beginning to rise before anyone says anything.

"Is there actually anything you can do to help

John?" Terrell asks. "I mean, anything to keep her out of harm's way?"

"I can't think of anything at all. Absolutely nothing," I say.

"Okay, this may seem far-fetched, but hear me out. When would you be due to go out on that ship of yours again?"

"Not sure, I'd guess a little under a week. Why?"

"How about getting your old job back, and smuggling her on board? You'd then at least have three months to figure out a plan or something."

I'm stunned. Terrell is always the quiet one, he never says much, he's just always there and always on your side. But every now and then, something pops out of his mouth that seems to be the solution to all the problems in the world. And he may well have just solved mine. Possibly, anyway.

"I could fucking kiss you," I say.

"Not in front of Jacob's mum you won't."

"My job may be gone though. Less than a week to go before *Sunspot 2* goes out again? They've got to have replaced me by now."

Jacob looks up and smiles his sly little smile.

"You said that you didn't do anything in your job, and that it was pointless you being there as the crew pretty much manages itself, right?" he says.

"Yeah, what are you getting at?"

"You also said your boss begged you to stay, and he also said he'd hold it open for as long as possible, right?"

"Yes," I say slowly.

"It's still waiting for you. I guarantee it. He's not even tried to replace you. The ship would function fine without you or a replacement. Did you even tell anyone on your shift that you were leaving?"

"Come to think of it, no."

"That's harsh man. But then, if you get your job back tomorrow, they'll never know what a heartless dick you are."

I smile at that. One small problem does start spinning around in my mind though. If I do get my job back, and make arrangements to somehow smuggle her aboard, what if she doesn't want to go? What if she'd rather stay and face the consequences than escape with me?

"What if she doesn't want to?" I ask. There is a long pause. Finally Jacob puts his hand on my shoulder.

"Cross that bridge when you come to it John. Just sort the other shit out first."

28

I can't sleep. Jacob's sofa just isn't big enough to sleep on. I'm either dangling my legs off the end, or bending my knees until they ache. Either way I see every hour pass by on the glowing clock on the wall. At about six am Terrell walks in and turns all the lights on. I wasn't expecting it and I cover my eyes. I hear him moving around in the kitchenette for a few minutes and then he moves in to the lounge and turns on the holobox. He sits in the armchair and watches the news while he eats his breakfast and drinks his coffee.

"Morning John," he says as if this is normal.

"What the fuck are you doing?" I ask, annoyed. "It's six in the morning."

"Getting ready for work. This is my morning routine."

I'd been so absorbed in my situation that it hadn't

even occurred to me that Jacob and Terrell still have jobs to go to in the daylight hours. But they still come out every night if I ask, and even if I don't.

"Oh shit, sorry," I say sitting up, but keeping the duvet on me. I stare blankly at the screen for a few minutes, not taking anything in before I decide to get up and make a coffee. I hear Jacob get up. He walks into the lounge in just his boxers.

"Morning fuckers," he says, stretching. With the amount he drinks and smokes and generally abuses his body, I can't work out for the life of me how he manages to maintain a six pack.

"Do you want a coffee?" I ask him, already getting a second cup out.

"Why not?" he says, now sitting on the sofa and staring at the box.

"Big day for you today John. Lots to sort out, lots to do. You'll be living in grovel city," he says to me, still staring at the box.

"I know. I think Mr. Hooper will be fine, but it's that slimy bastard Simon I have deal with first. God that guy's a prick. He'll do everything he can to make me squirm."

Terrell gets up, puts his cup and plate in the reclaimer and looks at me.

"You want a lift to your place to pick up your stupid scoot, or do you want to go straight to the *Sunspots* loading yard?" I have a quick think.

"Probably mine. I'll just quickly get washed and

dressed."

"Coffee coffee coffee!" Jacob shouts over the back of the sofa at me. I quickly finish making it, pass him the cup and he downs it in one. His throat must be made of the same material as the heat shields on *Sunspot 2*.

"Cold and fucking awful," he shouts. Maybe not then. I take a sip of mine, and it's very cold.

"Sorry, I don't know how your machine works. I've gotta run," I say, walking quickly to the bathroom.

Terrell drops me off outside my house and I wonder if I should go in and see if Ez is inside. I look down at what I'm wearing and I know I can't go grovelling to my boss for my job back looking like this. There's no real choice. I have to go in. I walk up the drive and put my hand on the pad. The door opens and I make my way inside.

"Ez?" I say as I walk through the kitchen into the lounge. Nothing. I go upstairs, looking through the doors of each room. She's not here. Maybe she's gone to stay with friends, or worse, maybe with her parents. That'll complicate things.

I get changed into my best interview suit and head out to Bruce.

"Hello Bruce," I say to the slightly ridiculous vehicle, its door then opens up and I get in.

"Hello John, where are you headed today?" it asks me in a monotone.

"*Sunspots* loading yard, please."

"Would you like me to drive, or would you like to do it manually?"

"I'll drive today, thanks, Bruce."

Pulling out of the drive, I set off down the road in the direction of the motorway and the yard. I decide to take the upper level as it's got twelve lanes and always seems a little quieter than the five laned lower level. Bruce maxes out at two hundred kph, but cars are still speeding past me at almost double that. Bruce is perfect for town driving, but it's almost embarrassing how slow he goes on the motorways. There are one or two other vehicles available to buy that are slower, but not by much.

I get to the junction I need and cross the deceleration barriers onto the slipway and down onto the main road that heads to the yard. After a few minutes of country lanes I see the entrance. I pull up at the gates and Sally comes to the window of the booth.

"Hey John. Bit early aren't we? Your shuttle don't go up 'til Friday," he says, and presses something I can't see. The red force field drops and he waves me through. So far, so good. I guess Sally didn't get the memo. I drive to the staff car park and then head to the main office through the loading docks I used to work. I get the odd wave from one or two of the forklift drivers but that's it. It's a place I haven't been for a long time, as the shuttle bay is in the opposite direction. I obviously wasn't a very memorable employee.

The office block is ahead of me, a huge four story glass building beyond the docks. It still looks brand new and completely out of place. Everything around it is old and worn out and in desperate need of replacement. It's easy to see where the money is spent here. I get retina scanned and the main door opens. I would have thought my records would have been erased by now and that I'd have to be buzzed in, but no. Straight in. I walk through the short corridor to the reception and lean against the desk.

"Is it possible to see Mr. Hooper?" I ask the overly made-up but still stunningly attractive receptionist. She looks up and her purple irises turn pale blue and spin one eighty degrees. There's a small beep.

"No, he's in a meeting until twelve. Mr. Prelude is in, would you like to see him instead?" she asks and smiles vacantly. Simon. Fuck. I'd hoped to see Mr. Hooper first, but now I'm going to have to crawl through glass to get what I want, and still probably not get it. I sigh.

"Yeah, that's fine I guess. When is he available?" I ask.

Her irises change colour again, this time to yellow with another quiet beep.

"Hello ... yes, I've got someone here to see you, yes ... yes ... ." She looks straight at me. Her yellow eyes are unsettling. "Who can I say you are?"

"John Farrow."

"John Farrow ... yes ... yes ... fine, I'll let him know." Beep. She looks at me again and her eyes turn back to purple.

"He says ten minutes, please take a seat over there." She gestures towards the bench opposite her desk and I sit down.

I'm sitting there waiting for over an hour. I don't question it, if he wants to play his little power games I'll just let him do it. If he needs to use his authority to try and make me feel small and insignificant, I'll just play along. After about an hour and a half the receptionist looks up.

"He'll see you now," she says pointing up the stairs. Standing up from the wooden bench, I stretch out, realise that my arse has got pins and needles, and then awkwardly ascend.

His office door is open when I get to it, but I knock on it anyway as he's looking down at some paperwork. It's been a while since I've seen him, but he still looks like a stick insect.

"Come in come in, take a seat," he says. I do. He looks at me with a half-smile. "What can I do for you, Mister ... ?" I just stay silent and let it hang in the air. He knows my name. He's just trying to make himself feel important. He doesn't get involved with the little people. I really need to play along, stroke his ego, make him feel like he is all powerful. But sometimes, someone is just such an enormous prick that you almost can't. Even when there's so much at stake. I take a breath and let my pride go.

"Farrow, John Farrow," I say finally.

"Ah yes, John. One of *Sunspot 2*'s shift managers. What can I do for you?"

I'm a little bit confused. I'm here to ask for my job back, but so far it seems that no one knows that I've left. When Martin Hooper said that he'd leave my position open, did he just mean that he wouldn't tell anyone and hope I'd return? Maybe Jacob was right. I'm going to have to tread a little bit carefully now and come up with some other reason why I'm here.

"I'm ... um ... here about the ... holiday entitlement ... ?" I say. It's the first thing that comes to my head.

"What holiday entitlement? You don't get holiday. You get three months out of every six off. Why on earth would you need any more? And besides, that's for the HR department," he says, sounding annoyed. I don't have anything else. My mind has gone completely blank. But then I realise I don't have to play his game anymore, and relax.

"Oh Simon, I don't want to talk to you anymore. It's Mr. Hooper I came to see. You're just an awkward little man who gets perverse pleasure out of being a dick. And you really are a dick." I can't believe that just came out of my mouth. He looks at me wide eyed and his face starts to turn red. He bangs a button on his personal computer and a disembodied hologram of the receptionist's head appears above his desk.

"Chantelle, get me Martin now," he barks at her. He's physically shaking.

"He's in meetings until twelve. I can't do … ."

"Get him now! I don't care about his meetings. He'll want to hear what John has just said to me." He hangs up and looks back at me. "I've been trying to make it happen for the last three years, but finally you've done something that I can actually get you sacked for."

I smile at him and put my hands behind my head.

"Oh, so you've tried to get me sacked before? I thought you didn't know who I was a few minutes ago," I say smugly. Too smugly.

"You've done it now. You've bloody done it now, I can't wait to see the look on his face."

I just continue to smile at him and he seems to be getting redder and redder. Simon then looks up and I hear the door bang open and the boss explodes into the room.

"How many times have I told you to never disturb me in meetings Simon?!" he booms.

"Sorry, sir, but I thought you should hear this straight away," he says and looks at me. "What did you say to me John? Or have you gone all shy now Mr. Hooper is here?" He smiles his evil little smile. Martin looks down at me. I stand up and shake his hand.

"Hello John," he says. "It's really good to see you."

"And you sir," I reply. Simon starts to look a little

bit flustered.

"No ... John tell him what you said to me, or I will."

Martin looks at him.

"Oh be quiet, Simon. Stop flapping around like a pompous arse." He looks back at me. "What can I do for you John?"

"I'm really sorry for messing you around and everything sir, but my circumstances have radically changed, and I was wondering if I could have my old job back?" He looks at me and smiles. Simon looks from me to Martin and back with a look of shock and incomprehension on his face.

"Of course, John, of course. I was hoping this would happen. Talk about cutting it fine though, the shuttle leaves tomorrow night," he booms with laughter at that for some reason, and bangs me hard on the shoulder. With that, he walks out. I look back at Simon, and can tell he's trying to say something, but he can't find the words. His mouth keeps opening and closing and his left eye is twitching. I just smile, flip him the bird and walk out. My heart is pumping fast when I get back to Bruce. That situation could have gone either way. I was very lucky Mr. Hooper hadn't told anyone and had held out for me or I would have been screwed. And fucking over Simon felt good, even if was stupid and reckless.

I get Bruce to drive and I give Jacob a call.

"All sorted, my job is mine again. Now for phase

two of the plan. I've got to find Ez and get her to come with me somehow," I say.

"She wasn't at your place then?" he asks.

"No, but I'm going back there now. She may have just not been there this morning ... ." I pause. Suddenly a cold chill comes over me.

"What if *Skylark* have gotten to her already?"

"No John, it's fine. Just get there as quickly as you can."

I try her phone but don't get an answer. I'm not sure she'd answer me anyway so that doesn't prove anything. I get back home and have another look around. This time I check the drawers and the wardrobe in our bedroom. Most of her stuff is gone. At least that's good news. Hopefully. I go through the contacts on my phone and call anyone it's likely she might stay with but no one's seen her. Or so they claim. This now means I'm going to have to go to her parents and see if she's there. If she is, this isn't going to go well. They hate me, and if she's told them what's going on, they will have paid for a private security company to guard her at all times and they most definitely won't let me see her. I've got to try though. And when better than now? So I get back in Bruce and set a course.

29

Ez's parents live in a massive manor house on the outskirts of the city. When you're there it feels like you're in the middle of nowhere, but it's only ten minute drive from civilisation. They're pretty fucking rich. Her dad is the president of *the New White Star*, an intergalactic cruise ship company. Did I mention they hate me? I think I did but it's worth re-iterating that fact. I pull up to their gatehouse at around four pm; the sun is beginning to set and the gate is shut with a guard posted. I get out of Bruce and start to walk over to the guard. His raises his rifle and aims it squarely at my head. I put up my hands.

"Wait wait wait, I'm just here to see Ez," I say, hoping to get him to give me some indication as to whether she's here or not. The guard doesn't say a word, but primes his rifle and it starts humming.

"Okay, okay. I'm John Farrow, I'm Ez's partner, I only want to help, but I'll go," I say and start to head back to Bruce.

"Wait," the guard says walking over to an intercom. Another guard takes his place and points his rifle at me. After a minute or so the first guard comes back.

"I'm very sorry mister Farrow, but you are not welcome here. Leave, and never come back or you will be shot on sight. This is your only warning," he says loudly.

I think leaving is the definitely the best option for now; I don't really want to piss off anyone who's been ordered to shoot me dead. I get back into Bruce and drive away. I'm sure Ez must be inside, and I've got to see her. Sure, she's protected for now, but if *Skylark* decided to make a move the private security firm would be no match for them. *Sunspot 2* is the safest option. There's only one other entrance into Ez's parents property, and that's through a little travelled country road. I'd imagine that's guarded as well, so it's probably not worth trying to get in that way either. I'm not sure what the best plan of action is, I know the property fairly well so a night time raid would probably make the most sense. Get in over the perimeter wall, quietly sneak through the garden and up to the house, hope that Ez sees me before anyone else does. It's highly likely that she'll set off the alarm if she does see me, but I'm counting on the fact that she doesn't want to get me killed. Hopefully she'll listen. So many things can go wrong, but I'm all out of options. I'm going to have to get Jacob and Terrell involved, I can't do this by myself.

I head back home and grab a few things: clothes, a wash kit and a sleeping bag. I don't feel safe here after recent events and drive back to Jacob and Terrell's place. Terrell is sitting where he was this morning, as if he hasn't moved. This time he's eating pizza and drinking a beer instead of cereal and coffee. Jacob is still on the sofa staring at the holobox.

"We're going to have to get her tonight," I say to them. They both look at me, then at each other.

"Okay, as long as we're back by ten. I've got a hot date with Jayna and her boyfriend," Jacob replies. Terrell looks at him, feigns disgust by pretending to put his fingers down his throat, and then looks at me.

"What's the plan then?" he asks.

"I think simplicity is probably the key thing here. Her parents' house is being guarded by a private security company, and they've been told to shoot me on sight. Which, in my opinion is a bit rude. There are two gate houses, both guarded, and a ten foot wall around the whole property. So we find a quiet bit of wall, you guys bunk me over and I run like fuck." Terrell puts his hands over his face.

"That is a terrible plan," Jacob says. "You'll be shot as soon as you're on the other side of the wall. They're bound to have the whole place wired up with motion and heat detectors, and probably have a few *S and D drones* just to be on the safe side."

"You got any better suggestions?" I ask and there is a long silence. Clearly there aren't any. Finally Terrell takes his hands off of his face and talks.

"It just needs some finessing. Jacob and I are going to have to be decoys if you want this to work. You'll need one of us at both entrances causing enough mischief that the guards stop paying attention to their monitors, and want to kick the shit out of us instead. If they are using an *S and D drone*, I may know someone who can get me a device to temporarily confuse its sensors. That should give you a chance to get in and explain yourself. I'll give him a call now."

Terrell only knows one man that I know of who can get equipment like that. Tommy fucking Pritchard. And he's nut job. A charming nut job. In spite of myself, I do actually quite like him, but I don't trust him. He left the military after his basic training because he got home sick, but he's spent all his time since being out telling anyone who will listen that he was booted out because he didn't like to play by the rules. Unfortunately for me, he is a great source for getting used military hardware. When I say used, it usually hasn't been. He'll insist on coming along. I really don't want someone I can't trust involved in this, but annoyingly he's also the only person I know who could pull it off. Terrell then looks over to me.

"Tommy says he can get anything we need for tonight, but he's coming too," he says. I nod my head, knowing that I've just made a bad idea much worse. After a few minutes he hangs up.

"He wants us to meet him at the *Black Dog Café* in two hours. Tommy says he'll scope out the place and come up with a plan." Terrell then looks at Jacob. "Looks like you're gonna have to cancel your date night." Jacob looks genuinely upset.

"But it was going to be my first threesome," he says in a high pitched whine. He then smiles. "No sorry, make that my third threesome. But it would have been my first with a man and a woman. The two guys were good, and two girls were great, but I wanted the full holy trinity of threesomes. I'm pretty greedy like that."

Two hours later the three of us are sitting in a small booth at the *Black Dog Café*. We're all wearing black, slowly drinking our coffees, and standing out somewhat. *Black dog, black clothes, black coffee.* Jacob opens his man bag, ruffles around a little and produces three small clear plastic tubes. Inside are what look like tiny mechanical spiders.

"When we start this crazy plan of yours, open the tubes and drop the *spiders* into your hands. Not for too long, or they'll melt. Quickly put them under or above your eye and they'll crawl in and attach themselves to your eyeball. They'll quickly absorb and you'll feel more focused than you ever have. I think it's the only way to do this right," he says.

"Are you sure? This doesn't sound like the best idea," I say, hoping that Terrell will join me in my half protest. But no.

"Shit, Jacob, I didn't know you had any of these," he says and looks at me. "Seriously John, these things are awesome. They don't change you or screw with your mind, they just make a better version of you. Quicker, stronger, more agile, they make you think faster."

I nod my head and agree, but have a horrible feeling that everything is going to turn to shit. I hear the door of the cafe slide open and Tommy walks in wearing full camouflage and a blue cap. The waitress looks up at him, smiles to herself and walks back to the till. He then walks over and starts talking to her. I don't hear what's said, but the conversation abruptly ends with her telling him to fuck off. He then sits on our table with a wide toothy grin. I think this is maybe the reason I don't trust him. Not his misogyny, but his teeth. They are black, brown, and rotting away with loads missing. How in this day and age is it possible to have teeth that bad? It makes my skin crawl just looking at them, so I look away.

"I'm all set up. The area is all scoped out. They only have one *search and destroy drone* roaming the grounds, it's an older model with tripod legs instead of the force field to keep it up. And when I say keep it up, I don't mean my cock if you know what I'm saying."

I'd forgotten about his awful, but constant references to his manhood. Or probably lack of.

"I'll disable the drone from a distance, you three then do whatever it is you plan to do," he says, dropping three silver earpieces on the table. "Put those in your ears so we can communicate with each other and keep everything running smoothly. Any questions?" He looks around the table, grins again showing his horrible chimp teeth and claps his hands together. "No? Then let's head out."

We all pick up the earpieces and put them in place. Jacob then passes Tommy a *spider*. He looks at it, scrunches his face up for a few seconds, and then realises what it is.

"Fuckin' eh. There's no way we can fail now." He opens the lid of the tube and tips it directly into his eye. He closes it, shakes his head and bangs on the table with his fists.

"God fucking damn, I can feel that right down to my ball sack."

Jacob and Terrell do the same. I pretend to, but don't undo the lid and put the tube in my top pocket. I need to be sober for this. Not on some crazy drug I've never tried before. On a night out, most definitely. I'd take three or four. I just can't risk it now.

30

We leave the *Black Dog Café* together, but once we're out of the door we split up and head to our own cars and drive away to our separate destinations. Jacob to the main gate, Terrell to the back gate, Tommy up some hill he's found that has a decent view of the property, and I'm heading for the little woods that's on the perimeter of the property's south side. There is constant three-way chatter between Jacob, Terrell and Tommy through the earpiece. Terrell said that the spiders make a better version of you, but on the evidence of what they're saying to each other, they make complete dick versions of you.

"John, John, John, when I'm at the front gate I'm, I'm gonna pretend I'm lost, I'll tell the guard that the car's A.I. is broken and I have no idea where I am,"

Jacob says at double the speed he normally talks at.

"Good idea," I reply. "But what if he just tells you to get lost like he did to me earlier?"

"Don't worry, John," Tommy says. "I saw their shift change earlier, the night shift won't give a shit. They'll just be watching porn."

"Surely that'll make them more annoyed about being disturbed," I say.

"I wouldn't have thought so, John. Try not to worry so much. The lads know what they're doing. If there is a problem, there won't be for long. Not as long as my shlong anyway."

Jacob and Terrell burst out laughing at that comment, way more than it deserved. I seriously start to think about pulling the plug. This isn't how I wanted to do this. Three drugged up idiots, one who may or not be mentally unbalanced. But I have no time left. It's tonight or never.

I drive down the dusty country road towards the south side of the house and finally after lots of bends, which seem way worse at night. I get to the little lay-by next to the small woods. I pull in, turn Bruce's lights off and get out. Through the trees, I can just about make out the wall and the lights from the house above it, around a hundred metres away through the foliage. I un-bungee the small stepladder that I'd hastily put on Bruce's roof before we set out, and head off into the darkness towards the wall. As I slowly work my way through the trees and bushes with the stepladder on my shoulder, I'm really hoping I didn't scratch Bruce's roof. Not at all what I should be thinking or caring about right now, but it just pops in there. I reach the wall and lean the ladder against it and wait.

"I've got your heat signature in my sights, John," Tommy says at double speed in my earpiece. "We'll wait until the lads are in position and we'll get this party started."

"Yeah, that sounds like a plan," Jacob replies. "We'll head out after this, back to *Jupiter Rising*. I've got a good buzz going on right about now." I really can't take much more of this.

"I'm pulling the plug. This is fucked. Jacob, you said the spiders would help us, but all that's happening is you being a dick and wanting to party. This is important. One wrong move from you and you could be shot dead," I shout and whisper at the same time.

"Too late to pull the plug my good man, I've just pulled up at the front gate. Listen and learn." My heart beat speeds up to almost a drum roll. It's happening, it's actually happening. I hear Jacob's car door open, and hear his footsteps on the gravel. I can then hear a muffled voice shout at him.

"You're not permitted here, be on your way or I'm authorised to use deadly force," it says. There is a long pause, and I start to think that maybe Jacob's lost his nerve, but then he speaks.

"I'm lost mate, my car's *A.I.* has gone ape-shit. I

have no idea where I am. Can you show me on this map?" I hear the crinkling of paper. Has Jacob really brought a map with him? The muffled voice doesn't sound all that interested in helping.

"I'll give you ten seconds to get off of this property or I'll shoot you down," it says.

"That's not very nice," Jacob says.

"Ten …"

"I think you're being pretty unreasonable here."

"Nine …"

"I mean, it's not like you couldn't take a quick look."

"Eight …"

"I'm not moving until you at least point out roughly where we are."

"Seven …"

"Seven?! Are you really going to count all the way down?"

"Six … I'm not kidding here, I will shoot you if you don't leave."

"But we were getting on so well, it'd be a shame to spoil it."

"Four …"

"You missed out five. Oh dear, I knew they got idiots in for security work, but you really do add an extra dimension to the word dumb." There are then two quick hissing noises.

"Front gate clear," Jacob says. I'm completely at a loss for what's just happened.

"Back gate clear too," Terrell replies. "I was silent but deadly."

"How have you done that so easily?" I ask, but I'm almost scared to know the answer.

"Wrist mounted tranquilliser darts. I didn't tell you because you would have said no. Don't worry, they won't know what's hit them. But they'll feel it when they wake up in an hour or so," Tommy says. I probably would have said no to them, but at the same time I wouldn't mind having one myself now. I am a little worried that we've now left Ez without anyone to protect her. I'm just going to have to make doubly sure she says yes to my plan.

"Your turn, John. The tripod drone is on the other side of the grounds, so get over that wall now."

Without thinking about it too much I climb the ladder to the top of the wall, hang off of the other side and drop down into a bush. Once clear from that I run to the closest tree for cover, have a quick look left to right then run across the lawn to the side door of the house. Ez had given me a key to this door before we moved in together, so I could get into the house and avoid her parents. I hope the locks haven't been changed, it's been a while. I pull out my key fob, choose the one with the blue tape around the top and slowly ease it into the lock and twist. With a click it opens and I'm inside.

I creep through the dark corridor, the staircase to the annexe is on my right, and the door to the first drawing room is on my left. It's slightly ajar and there is a dull light coming from inside. I gently push the door open, and look through. Embers glow in the fireplace, and a lot of things are piled up on the coffee table next to smaller of the two sofas. The room is empty, so I walk through the door and take a closer look at the mess. Fuck. There are two empty bottles of vodka on the table, a half-finished bottle of whiskey, and four used *Emergency Stops*. Not the club ones. Not the ten minute high ones. These are the slightly more illegal ones you get from the underworld. Unmodified, so they keep you in a fog for hours, then make you think you need to stay in that fog forever. I doubt these belong to Ez's parents. I'm about to leave and check elsewhere, when the door to the kitchen swings open and I can see Ez's silhouette. She's looking down at the floor and holding a bottle in each hand. She hasn't spotted me yet, and walks in towards the coffee table. She then stops dead, and drops both bottles on the floor, one smashes and the other one bounces. In one quick movement she pulls a pistol out of a holster that I hadn't spotted attached to her jeans and points it at me. I put my hands up.

"It's me it's me, it's John," I say quickly before she decides to pull the trigger. She lowers the pistol a little bit.

"John ... why are you here? How ... how did you get in?" Considering what's on the coffee table, she sounds almost sober. Almost.

"There's no time to worry about that now. I've got to get you out of here, I've got a plan." I say, feeling a little bit like the hero rescuing a damsel in distress in an old film. She looks at me, stony faced.

"I'm not going anywhere with you, I'm here because I want to be away from you," she says.

"I know that. And I'm really sorry. Everything was a mess, and I didn't know what to do."

"I was in a terrible situation, and you didn't believe me. Instead of staying with me to help me through it, you just continued to go out every night with your friends."

"I couldn't get through to you."

"You didn't even try!" she snaps at me. "Once I started becoming a hindrance to you, you just carried on as if I wasn't even here. All I wanted was to be loved, to be comforted. Through thick and thin. Something that I thought you were capable of. But I'm not sure you are. I can see now that you're completely self-absorbed, not in a vain way because you're always a mess. You think the world revolves around you and you alone, and you've been doing your best to push me out of that world since Rupert disappeared. I loved you John, with all my heart I did. But you didn't believe me. You didn't believe me. And that's what hurts the most."

I look down at the floor. That hurt. None of it is necessarily untrue.

"I do now," I manage.

"It's too little too late. There is nothing left for you here now," she says and lifts the pistol back up.

"I've got a way to keep you safe," I say, knowing it's probably in vain, but knowing I've still got to try.

"I don't care. I am safe." She looks around.

"No, you're not. If I can get in here with almost no effort, how easy do you think it'll be for *Skylark* to?"

She doesn't answer.

"*Sunspot 2* sets out tomorrow night. I can get you on board, you'll be safe there with me for three months while we work out what to do."

"But you quit that job," she says.

"I got it back to save you."

There are a few seconds of silence.

"You want to save my life by doing the exact opposite to what I would have wanted?" she says, and then half smiles. "That pretty much sums up our relationship." She lowers the pistol.

"Will you come with me?" I ask, feeling hopeful.

"I'll let you know in the morning, and when my parents get back I'll let them know. I've got too much shit in my system to make a real decision now. The *Emergency stops* made me feel way too spaced out, so I topped them up with a couple of *Spiders*. I'm not sure that was such a good idea. I now feel spaced and anxious at the same time."

"That's a lot of shit in your system," I say.

"I was hiding. From everything. Like you've been

doing the last three months. Let me walk you out."

Ez walks me back through the corridor, when we reach the side door she kisses me on the cheek.

"I'm glad you're finally on my side," she whispers.

"I'm an idiot, but I catch up eventually." I smile a childish smile and walk out of the door backwards, staring at Ez's gorgeous, pale face. Her expression suddenly changes from a half smile, to horror. I turn around and the tripod sentry drone appears from behind the annexe, it raises its weapons and shines a red light in my face.

"Run back inside, John! You're not cleared! It's programmed to kill trespassers on sight." I stand there stock still, I'm too scared to move.

"Don't worry John, I've got this," Tommy says through my earpiece, and within a split second the head of the four and a half metre tall behemoth explodes. I cover my eyes but a wall of heat hits me and I'm thrown to the ground. I open my eyes, and see what's left of the three legged metal monster collapse to the ground, trailing thick black smoke from where its head should have been. My ears are ringing and I feel slightly dazed. I stand up and start to head back towards the house, but Ez is no longer in the doorway. I look around, and see her running down the driveway towards her scoot, Brucette. I realise that she must think *Skylark* have destroyed the drone to get to her, and she's decided to leg it. This is not good. I try and run after her, but she's got in and started driving before I get anywhere near. I'm going to have to get to Bruce and go after her, try and get her to stop and let her know everything's alright. But before that, I'm going to have to catch up with her, and she's an aggressive driver. That will probably mean the most embarrassing car chase in history. Before I can even turn and head back to the wall, it looks like she starts to lose control. Brucette then veers off of the driveway and hits one of the carved marble markers that run down the sides of it up to the main gates. Brucette rolls about four times, and the carbon fibre skin is torn away, just leaving the framework and inner workings visible.

I run as fast as I can shouting Ez's name, but the air ambulances that are always within a minute or two of any accident get there just before I do. I'm guessing Tommy must have put a call in. A medic comes running up to me.

"What happened, sir?" he asks me as I get to the scene.

"She was scared ... she was running ... ." I'm still too shell shocked to put together a sentence. The other two medics already have Ez out of the wreckage and on to a stretcher. I stare at her, she's not moving but she doesn't look damaged. Just a little blood coming out of her nose and left ear.

"Is she ... ."

"No, she'll be okay. We just need to get her to the hospital, and fast. Sir, is there anything more you can tell me about her condition?" I stare at the medic blankly and he starts to walk back to the ambulance.

"Tell him about the drugs she's taken, John," Terrell shouts through my earpiece.

"Drugs," I blurt out. The medic turns.

"What sort?"

"Um ... *Emergency Stops*, *Spiders* and vodka. A lot." He nods and runs into the back of the ambulance. The rear doors raise and it takes off, quickly leaving me alone and in silence.

31

The four of us are sitting in the hospital waiting room. Jacob, Terrell and Tommy must be on a come down by now, they're all looking pale and clammy in the harsh florescent lights, but they don't complain about it. It's been three hours since the accident, and a massive part of me wants to lay the blame right at Tommy's feet. But I can't. He saved my life. It was my own fault for not looking where I was going. It just kick started a chain of events that spiralled out of control. I look around the room. These are my best friends. I'm lucky to have them. Who else would have gone through that to help a friend in need? I'm not even sure I would. I am a lucky man.

"Thank you," I say. "You guys don't have to stay though. You can go home, it's really late."

"No worries, John, we're with you until the end,"

Jacob says and smiles. The waiting room door opens and a doctor comes in.

"John Farrow?" he asks, and I stand up.

"Come with me please." I follow him out into the corridor.

"How is she?" I ask sheepishly.

"She was very, very lucky. The amount of drugs in her system and the stress caused her to have a cardiac incident, and we believe that's the reason she crashed. We have fixed that. Unfortunately, the sudden impact of the crash, and the insignificant safety features in that little vehicle of hers has fractured her skull. She's also got a swelling on her brain, so we're going to have to keep her in a coma until it goes down."

That all sounds pretty awful.

"But the good news is that the baby is fine."

At least there is some good news … .

"Wait, what are you talking about?" I ask, feeling flustered.

"The baby is going to be fine. According to her charts she's about three months pregnant."

"Her charts? She's been in about this? Three months … ?"

"Yes she has, and as I said, everything is fine in that respect." The doctor continues talking, but I can no longer hear him. I don't know what to do. My brain feels like it's going to explode with this information. She's known all this time. The conversation we had by the river before *Jupiter Rising* was just testing the water. She already knew that I was going to be a stay at home dad, that's why she wasn't pushing for me to get another job. She was letting me get it all out of my system before she finally told me the truth. Would I have known about it by now if her boss hadn't have gone missing? Should I have guessed? I don't know. But since then she's been treating her body like a chemical waste facility. She knew all of this and still kept filling herself with drugs and alcohol. I feel betrayed. She's betrayed our unborn child. I fucking hate her for this. Everything that I thought I knew is wrong. I can't stay here any longer. I have to get away. I turn from the doctor and walk out of the hospital. Before I know it, I'm driving Bruce towards the *Sunspots* loading yard and the shuttle bay that will take me back to *Sunspot 2*. Part of me knows it's a terrible decision that I'll probably regret, but in the red mist of anger I can't stop myself.

32

My eyes begin to slowly open, and the lights above me are blurry and blinding. My head is throbbing and I try to move my hand in front of my face to block out the light but I can't move my arm. I can't move either of them, they seem to be tied up behind me. My feet are tied too. I open and close my eyes quickly to try and get my vision back and realise I'm sitting tied to a chair next to one of the thin ends of the pool table in the rec deck. Robert is sitting to my left on one of the long sides, he's slumped and still unconscious. Kerry is opposite him on the other side, also unconscious. Mark is sat opposite me on the far end, wide eyed and silent.

"What's going on?" I ask.

"I don't know. The lights were red. They then went back to normal. I went to find Robert, but something got me. I woke up here about ten minutes ago and you were all here too. We're all going to die, John."

I try and pull my hands out of the rope, but they're

not moving. I'm stuck.

"Can you get free?" I ask.

"No, been trying since I woke up. They won't budge."

Kerry starts to stir, and I call her name quietly a few times. Her eyes open wide and her head moves up sharply. She tries to move her arms without success.

"What the fuck is happening?!" she shouts, looking at me.

"I don't know," I say. "But we're completely screwed."

Kerry looks at Mark.

"I'm so sorry about earlier," he says to her. "I was completely out of order." He looks like he really means it.

"Don't worry about it, you daft bastard. They say make up sex is better than standard sex anyway." He smiles, but his face then drops as I guess he remembers where we are.

Kerry looks at Robert who's still slumped over.

"Oi, wake up you fat fuck," she shouts, and he wakes up with a jolt. He then proceeds to do the same thing the rest of us have done and tries to pull his hands free of the rope.

"What the ... ?" he says.

"No good Robert. We're stuck here." she says to him. I look from Kerry to Mark, to Robert and back to Kerry. I think it's safe to say we're all terrified.

"Who's done this to us?" Robert asks.

"Or what has," I reply.

He looks at me with what looks like confusion, anxiety and terror all at the same time. He then turns to Kerry, I guess for verification of the *what*.

"What we found on the hangar. It was fucked up," she says.

"What did you find?" Mark asks. I let Kerry say it, it's more likely that they'll listen to her.

"We found Tom. His neck was ripped right fucking open. In fact, his head was almost off," she says.

Robert looks at Mark, both have the same expression of horror on their faces.

"That's not all. Underneath his neck, was a load of translucent slime. John found the same stuff earlier when he was in the inspection tubes, and the cargo bay."

"Holy shit," Robert says under his breath.

"We're all going to die," Mark says again.

"There was a wooden transport crate as well, we opened it, but John and I didn't have any idea what it was."

Robert and Mark are just staring at us.

"What killed Tom then? Did you find the rest of his shift?" Mark asks, and looks at me.

"No, we didn't. I don't know what's happened to them. I get the feeling we won't have to wait very long to find out," I reply.

"Are we all on the same page here?" Robert asks.

"Are we all thinking that something extra-terrestrial may have done this?"

"Yes, we're all thinking fucking aliens. As ridiculous as that sounds," Kerry says.

No one says anything for a while, and we all continue to try and free ourselves. I've been constantly struggling since I woke up, and my wrists are starting to burn with the effort. I start to feel a trickle of something down my hand, blood I'd imagine, so I decide to stop struggling and slump. Kerry looks at me.

"Are you giving up?" she asks.

"I might be. I'm not sure I see the point anymore. Mark's right, we're all going to die."

"Fucking stop it. You're head has been up your arse this whole trip John, you've not been yourself. You may as well tell us what happened to you before this trip. What you hinted at after the fire in the engine room, but then pussied out of. Tell us why you're here when you're not supposed to be."

So I do. I lay myself bare. I tell them everything. There is a long silence after I've finished. It finally gets broken by Robert.

"That's harsh, man."

"I know it was, but I couldn't make sense of it. My head just fogged up and I didn't think any of it through. She couldn't deal with the stress, so she hid away from everything with drugs and drink. I just ran away. I left her alone and unprotected in a hospital bed, in a coma. I didn't even see her. *Skylark* could easily take her out. Her, and my unborn child. It doesn't seem real. I wouldn't have thought it was possible for me to do that. They could be dead. It's all I can think about. It just goes around and around in my head. And the more I think about it the worse I feel."

"And you should feel bad. I didn't think you could be that person, John. I thought you were one of the good ones. But you can't give up. There's still a good chance she's alive. You have to keep hold of that, you can't give up. Not after what we've been through today. You have to get back for her," Kerry says, her eyes pleading with me.

"That was my plan, in the hangar anyway. But look at us now. Look around the table at our sorry faces. We're done. We all know it. I've given up because I've got nothing left."

"Then you deserve your misery," she says.

There is sound from the next level up. The door to someone's quarters gets slammed closed, and I hear footsteps.

"Shhhhhh, listen," Robert says quietly. The familiar sound of feet hitting the rungs of the ladder comes from behind him. I look to my left and see two legs emerging from the hatch above, taking one slow step at a time. We're all transfixed, but Robert is facing the cargo bay, and can't see anything.

"What is it? What is it?" he asks quietly. But no one

answers him. We just watch the figure slowly climb down. When it finally hits the deck, it turns around to face us. Kerry then looks at Robert.

"It's wearing a suit. It's wearing a fucking suit," she says to him.

It is indeed wearing a suit, but also some sort of paper bag on *its* head with uneven eyeholes cut out. *It's* a man. A man wearing a homemade paper bag on his head. He walks towards us, his shiny black shoes click against the metal deck plates as he moves. *Click ... Click ... Click ... Click ...* As he gets closer I can see that the bag on his head has lines of printed text with diagrams on it. The bag itself has been badly stuck together with tape. He stops about two metres behind Robert.

"Hello, I trust everyone's comfortable," he says in a smooth unfamiliar voice.

"Who the fuck are you supposed to be, you paper headed prick?" Kerry asks him. He points at his head.

"This? Do you not like it? I made it myself out of an instruction manual," *Paper headed prick* says in his slightly creepy monotone. He then starts to walk around the pool table anti-clockwise. *Click ... Click ... Click ... Click ...* I feel the air move as he walks behind me, he then passes Kerry and runs his fingers through her pink hair. As he walks behind Mark, Mark flinches. *Paper headed prick* stops behind Robert and puts his hands on his shoulders. Robert's eyes open wide, and he looks like he may have a heart attack. He moves his head to Robert's ear.

"Everything was going so very smoothly. It was quickly put together, but there was no reason for it to go wrong. But he was a snooper. He snooped. He found out. I had no choice after that. No choice." He lets go of Robert's shoulders and continues to circle the pool table. *Click … Click … Click … Click …* Robert lets out a sigh of relief.

"What the fuck are you talking about?" Kerry shouts. He runs his fingers through her hair again as he walks behind her.

"There's no reason you'd understand. You were the only one here who had a chance at stopping me. But you didn't. You know too much. But so little." *Click … Click … Click … Click …*

"You're a fucking nut job mate," she sneers.

"Sticks and stones. I don't think you'd be the same person if you came home to find your wife and children burned alive."

Mark looks up.

"Your wife and children were murdered?" he asks quietly.

"A kidnapping gone wrong. An attempt to control me. Oh but my wife knew how to put up a good fight. They didn't expect that. In the end her ability to fight got her nowhere of course. Just dead. Unfortunately the stupid bitch got my children killed too. And my beloved dog. I can't really blame her. I brought it all on myself by being difficult." *Click … Click … Click*

... Click ...

"Why did you kill Tom?" I quietly ask as he walks behind me. "And where's the rest of his shift?" He stops and puts his mouth up to my left ear.

"John finally speaks," he whispers, his warm breath tickles my earlobe and makes me feel queasy. He then moves away and continues his circling. *Click ... Click ... Click ... Click ...*

"Everybody, John has spoken!" he shouts. "It's nice to finally meet you John. John and I go way back. Best friends John and I. John. John. John. You gave me the inspiration, John. I love it when we talk like this John."

"You know each other?" Robert sheepishly asks. *Paper headed prick* looks in his direction, and then picks up a yellow pool ball from the table. He throws it at full force towards Robert's head. It misses by less than a centimetre. The ball bounces off of the wall, and clatters to a halt on the patterned deck plates. *Paper headed prick* walks over to it and picks it up.

"I thought I'd be a better shot than that. I guess that sums up the last few weeks. I'm not great at everything." He walks towards Robert throwing the ball from one hand to another, and I notice that he seems to have an erection.

"What to do, what to do," he mutters to himself and then holds the ball in the air about a metre above Robert's head and drops it. Robert screams in agony as it bounces off of his shaved tattooed skull and back on to the deck plates.

"I don't think that was a big enough lesson." *Paper headed prick* walks over to where the cues are racked up and grabs one with his right hand and gently slaps his left with it. He slowly moves behind Robert and stands still about a metre behind him. Robert has his eyes closed, and is slightly rocking back and forth. *Paper headed prick* just stands there, not moving or saying anything. I can see that Kerry is about to say something, or probably shout something at him, when *Paper headed prick* raises his finger to where his mouth should be.

"Shhh," he says. "The thing about a lesson, is that people take different things away from it. This is a lesson I want you to all take away the same thing from, the same meaning. No mixed messages." He swings the pool cue and with a loud slapping noise strikes Robert across the upper back and neck with it, again and again. After about nine or ten horrifying hits, the cue snaps and *Paper headed prick* drops it on the deck. Robert slumps forward.

"No more interruptions."

Kerry stares at *Paper headed prick* with pure hate, I've never seen her look like this. Mark has closed his eyes and is muttering something under his breath. My heart is beating fast, and I can feel the edges of fear, but mostly I'm just feeling numb.

"You didn't answer my question," I finally say. He looks back at me.

"And Robert here didn't let me finish telling everyone how we came up with this together, you and me. Me and you."

"You're mad. I've never met you."

"Of course you have, here I am." He slowly and carefully pulls off his paper bag mask and throws it on the green felt of the pool table. He smiles.

"Tim ... ? But you're dead. You were crushed," I say.

"Obviously I'm not. It was a high risk strategy, but once you'd shut the tube's hatch behind me, I simply moved down into one of the lower inspection tubes and waited it out. You didn't check there. I was a bit worried about the fire, and also the lack of oxygen when you opened the airlock. If you hadn't re-pressurised the engine room when you did, we wouldn't be having this pleasant conversation now. But yes, also I am dead. You see Tim was never alive, he was a fiction. A character I was playing. I tried to be as accurate as possible to someone on the lower levels of society. I put on the voice of a standard working man, made up a tiny bit of history, enough to be able to answer some rudimentary questions, and I blended right in." He stops and looks around the table smiling, he then starts to walk around it again anti-clockwise. *Click ... Click ... Click ... Click ...*

"What amuses me the most, is how none of this should have happened. I was quite happy to let the trip go as planned. You would have been none the wiser, and soon you'd all have been at home and cold with your loved ones. But Tom, Tom and his reports and his snooping. He ruined everything, and I had to think on my feet. He must have followed me onto the hangar. I didn't see him. He didn't know what I was up to, so he snooped. He saw me switch it on. Everything changed when that happened." *Click … Click … Click … Click …*

He walks behind Kerry and runs his hand through her hair. Every time he does a lap of the table he does it again, and I can see the impotent rage building up in her.

"The people at the loading docks are too easy to buy off. Once I'd met with your fat benefactor Martin Hooper, showed him my CV full of lies, told him I had some money and would do the first trip for free as a trial run, he couldn't give me the job fast enough. Then straight to the docks to see if I could procure a container to go on board. Everyone down there was in on this little side line. Just throw enough cash in their direction and you can dispose of anything. Little people fighting for scraps. But it served my purpose well enough." *Click … Click … Click … Click …* He runs his fingers through Kerry's hair again.

"Fucking stop that," she hisses at him.

"I probably won't. And it sounds to me like you haven't learned a thing from my little lesson. I don't like being interrupted. Besides, I haven't got to the best bit yet." He stares at me while continuing to walk.

Click ... Click ... Click ... Click ...

"Have you ever killed a man, John?" I look back at him, still not knowing why he's so interested in me. What have I done to pique his interest?

"No."

"Neither had I until earlier. It turns out to be an exquisite feeling. At first I didn't want to go through with it, I wasn't sure that I could. But when I thought about what I would lose if I didn't, I realised that I had to. As Tom was peering into the crate asking questions for his report, I used this knife." He pulls a sixteen centimetre hunting knife out of his inside jacket pocket.

"And I sliced it through his throat. With the micro chain blade it was like cutting through butter. I could feel a slight resistance as it cut through his jugular and windpipe, and I did it slowly to savour the feeling. The amount of blood surprised me, it sprayed in all directions. I've never felt so powerful, John, so sexually aroused. I couldn't help it, I had to release my seed onto his still twitching, gushing corpse."

I can see that he's got an erection again just thinking about it. I feel shell shocked and sick as I suddenly realise what the slime around the ship was. I can't believe I didn't realise. My numbness has gone, and the edges of fear come crashing down all around me. No one deserves to die like that. He walks past Kerry again, this time instead of running his fingers though, he pulls her hair tight and cuts a chunk out of it with his dry blood stained blade and throws it in the air. With pure rage she uses her whole body to try and shake herself loose from the chair, but as before, she still can't get free.

"You stay the fuck away from her!" Mark shouts desperately.

"What exactly are you going to do to stop me?" Mark stares at him with fire in his eyes, but Tim stares back and the fire quickly goes out. Mark drops his head and doesn't reply. Tim continues around the table. *Click ... Click ... Click ... Click ...*

"I then had to go about getting rid of the rest of his shift, there would be too many questions, too much snooping, and I really didn't need any more of that. Sam was alone in the engine room, she was a very pretty thing. It was shame. I told her Tom wanted to see her on the bridge. When she was with Will and Ian, I shut the hatches and trapped them all up there. From the console in the cargo bay I opened the bridge airlock and they were all blown out into space. Bye bye, no more questions, no more snooping. I then had to go about getting rid of the evidence. I'm quite proud of this, as I was now carving new ground, making it up as I was going along. I re-pressurised the bridge and looked for something I could use, plans or blueprints but the computers were empty, no schematics, nothing at all. I went into your office and found the maintenance manual, or the *bloody instruction manual* as you called it

John. It was gathering dust at the bottom of a cabinet. It was so satisfying blowing the dust off of it though, it felt like I'd discovered a relic from another era. I ripped out the pages I needed and put it back where I found it. I closed the hatches behind me, because I felt that it would be good to leave you sleeping beauties a mystery to wake up to. With the ripped out pages I went about stopping the engines, releasing the hangar deck, and removing the release controls."

"And I guess you just happened to masturbate all over the ship to add weight to this mystery of yours, you sick bastard," Kerry says then spits on the pool table.

"Not exactly, it's more of a problem I've always had, but it did seem to work out that way. I think John knows the reason I did that." He looks at me and smiles. "He must have heard the rumours at least."

"Why didn't you kill us as well?" I ask, ignoring the connection that is beginning to pop into my head.

"You must know this by now John. There are two reasons I didn't kill you. One: I didn't think there was a chance that your sub-standard shift would be able get anything working again. Unfortunately, I underestimated your ability to make things much worse. And two: I have too much respect for Ez to kill you outright." I stare at him. The connections are shouting at me, I just don't want to join the dots.

"... You know Ez?" I ask, but pretty sure I know

the answer.

"I was in charge of *the project* we were working on. She was one of the best scientists I had working under me. She was the only person I worked with that I considered a friend."

"You're …"

"Rupert Rawling. I'll let that just hang there." He does, and the fear that was crashing around me starts to turn into a red mist.

"If she was such good a friend, why did you destroy her life by leaving?" I shout.

"Someone's found his confidence. Good, John, good. I didn't destroy her, how could I have. I wasn't this person then. If anyone did destroy her, it was *Skylark*. But I see that you're here, and not back on Earth helping her. I'm sure you must feel good about that." I just stare at him. I have nothing to say. Nothing to defend myself with.

"*The project* was my brainchild. It wasn't until it was nearly finished that I started to realise the implications of it and got cold feet. I was so absorbed with it, I couldn't think about anything except getting it done. Ez was involved with the project's subsystems, and didn't know what the final outcome would be. It was always best that way, everyone had plausible deniability. Except of course me, and those in charge of *Skylark's* weapons division."

"So that's what's in the hangar. A weapon? You did all of this to dispose of a fucking weapon?" I ask.

Loudly.

"A weapon? Unfortunately, no. It's so much more than just a weapon John, it's the first actual doomsday device. Never to be used, but always there to keep any threats at bay. When *Skylark* realised that I wasn't going to complete the project, they decided to kidnap my family and force me to finish it. But you now know how that ended. This situation, here and now really is completely your fault John. Ez told me what you did for a living, how you dump waste on the sun, how proud she was of you. She wouldn't shut up about you. It was always John this, John that. Look at you John, you didn't deserve that level of commitment or love. When *Skylark* killed my family, they lost all their leverage on me, and I may even have lost my mind for a while. I decided that I had to get myself, and the project onto your ship any way I could." Kerry looks up at Rupert.

"So, what John said was right then, you fucking prick," she says.

"No, quite the opposite. I don't want to destroy it. The *project* was code named the *Forever dark*. Once it's fired into the sun it will extinguish it within six months. Or make it go supernova. It was fifty fifty on the simulations. *Skylark* wanted something special. It was only a matter of time before they had control of all of the United Governments. This would have sealed the deal. No one would dare go against them. When they killed my family, I lost everything. I made the decision that they'd lose everything as well, everyone would lose everything. A race that could build something like this, deserves to be wiped out by it. But you four have ruined everything. You've managed to completely cripple the ship, and now there's no way for me to get the *Forever dark* to the sun. It was all going so well, and now I really don't know what to do next." Kerry's face drops, and she turns to look at me wide eyed. He doesn't know that the hangar is still set to dump the waste, he must assume we're just holding position, and waiting to be rescued.

"What's that, Kerry? You look like you have something to say," he says and walks around the table and stands behind her. *Click ... Click ... Click ... Click ...* I look around, Robert and Mark know nothing of this either. If I mention it, will it be enough to give us time? It's the only play I have.

"Rupert, I guess you don't know what happened when Kerry and I went on board the hangar deck, do you?" He looks at me and his eyes thin.

"Go on."

"We didn't want to go back, not after what we'd seen. This *Forever dark*, or whatever the fuck it's called, and what was left of Tom. Kerry set the hangar to dump everything when it hits its co-ordinates, and then it takes us back home. You're plan is still in play. Unless anyone wants to get suited up and do another space walk to the hangar's forward airlock and stop it," I say.

He stands up straight and smiles widely, and lets out a huge sigh of relief.

"Thank you, John, that has made my day. Am I correct in assuming that Kerry is the only one who could, if she went across there, stop it?" She nods her head.

"I could kiss you," he says to the back of her head and wraps his arms around her shoulders in a hug. He smiles and starts to pull away. I notice he's still holding the knife in his right hand, and in one quick motion he pulls it through her throat. Her eyes open wide as blood starts to seep from the wound, followed quickly by a constant spurt that covers the green felt of the table and splashes over Robert's face and beard. She lets out a quiet gurgling sigh, her head slumps, and she's gone.

"No!" Mark shouts, helpless to do anything. Rupert walks around the table and does the same to him. I watch as the life drains out of Mark's eyes, all the while Rupert is staring at mine. I look down at the bloody felt of the pool table, and then close my eyes. I've killed them both.

"What did you expect, John? Were you hoping that would buy you some time? Save your lives maybe? No. I was always going to kill you. Whether it be freezing to death on earth or here like this. You weren't going to survive this John, no one was."

I start to struggle with my bonds as he slowly walks

over to Robert. *Click ... Click ... Click ... Click ...* Robert seems to have given up entirely. He hasn't moved since the pool cue was repeatedly hit against his back and neck. Rupert puts his left hand on the top of Robert's tattooed head and slowly pulls it back, all the while looking at me. Suddenly, from nowhere Robert's hand moves up and grabs hold of Rupert's tie, and pulls it down with a jolt. Rupert's nose hits the edge of the pool table hard and explodes. He screams loudly and drops the knife. With a loud groan Robert stands up out of the chair he was tied up to and pushes it back. Rupert is now staggering backwards and holding his bloody face, Robert moves behind him and picks him up by the back of his trousers and the neck of his jacket and lifts him above his head. Rupert's arms and legs are flailing around in all directions as Robert just holds him there. He turns around and walks to the chair he was tied to, and with a sickening crack, Robert drops him on the back of it. With a terrifying scream Rupert falls to the floor, with his spine bent in on itself, but he's seemingly still alive. Robert picks up the knife and cuts my binds. Shakily I stand up, and survey the awful scene.

"It's over," Robert says to me, his face and beard covered in Kerry's blood. I stare at him. There's nothing else to do. I put my arms around him, and bury my face in his chest. He holds me back, and we allow ourselves a moment to break down.

There is a deep rumbling from below us, and the

lights start to flicker. We stand apart from each other, both realising what this means.

"Oh no, we've got to get to the bridge," I say. We waste no time climbing up there, to get away from the horror on the rec deck. We both look out of the tinted viewports as hundreds of seemingly tiny cubes are heading towards the sun's corona and one by one we watch them burn up. The sun then slowly starts to move out of view as the thrusters from the hangar set us on a course for home.

I pull out the chair from behind Kerry's console and drop down into it, and hold my head in my hands. Robert puts a hand on my shoulder, and then sits down at Mark's console. We don't talk. We don't need to. We're alive, and the rest of our crew is dead. I'm pretty much responsible. There is no upside. We are at least on our way home. But if Rupert's claims were true, we'll have nothing to go home to.

"The device wasn't finished," I say after a while, breaking the silence. "Maybe it didn't work. I didn't see anything out of the ordinary as the containers burned up."

"We'll hold on to that thought for now. I hope you're right, I really do, but we have other things to worry about now. Kerry and Mark. We have to say our farewells."

33

After the awful, soul crushing job of cleaning up the rec deck, we carefully place Kerry and Mark into the main escape hatch in the cargo bay. I felt obliged to be the one who looked through Kerry's quarters. In there I found a photo dated a month before we set out on this trip. It's of her and what appears to be a pair of young adults, a boy and a girl. They're all laughing and look like they're having fun. I welled up when I realised who they were, but was also glad to know that she had managed to patch things up with her children after all. I decide to put the photo in the body bag with her. I don't know if that's what she would have wanted, but it seems like the right thing to do.

Robert did the same for Mark, as they were close in and out of work. He found some medals for various sporting achievements that he'd got in his youth, but not much else. I don't even know if he had a family.

I slowly type in my code, and Robert and I watch as the body bags with our friends inside leave the ship for the very last time. We bow our heads, and think about everyone we've lost today. After a while, I close the outer doors and there is only one thing left for us to do.

I really hoped that he'd died while Robert and I were on the bridge watching the waste container dump. But we weren't spared this new horror. Now, even after everything he's done, neither of us has the stomach to kill him. His spine has been snapped, and he's paralysed from the waist down. We don't have the equipment or the drugs on board to ease his pain, and he's delirious with it. The only thing we've been able to do for him is leave him in a bath tub in the washroom, and periodically shower him off after he's pissed or shat himself. The high-pitched howling noises coming from that room make my blood run cold. I don't imagine he'll survive the extended journey home. At least, I hope he doesn't.

EPILOGUE

Robert has managed to get the radio working, but only one way. We can now receive signals, but not reply to them. The first couple of weeks of listening in everything was sounding good, there was nothing at all about the Earth cooling off.

We kept that hope alive until eventually there were reports of icebergs appearing in the Mediterranean and sinking cruise ships. After that, everything seemed to go crazy. We heard reports of nuclear explosions, countries going to war with each other, oceans completely freezing over and mass evacuations of the rich and powerful. Soon after, we lost the signal and there was nothing left but static.

For days after that, Robert tirelessly tried to fix it, until the realisation that it was working fine and there was no signal to receive anymore.

We really don't know what we'll find when we get home, but it's very likely that almost everyone we know and love has perished. I hold out hope that Ez's parents were rich enough to be among the few who managed to get their families evacuated. If Ez is still alive, I will spend the rest of my days trying to find her.

I don't think I can hold out the same hope for Jacob and Terrell though. Even with Tommy around, who's a born survivor, I can't see any way they could have made it. I'd like to imagine they saw the world out in a drink and drug fuelled haze. The thought makes me smile, and that's how I want to remember them.

Even though the worst has happened, and I've been forced into spending the rest of my possibly short life with Robert, a spiteful bastard who is now my only friend, and a crippled mad scientist who took it on himself to end everything, I'm actually glad to be alive.

Who'd have thought it?

Thank you very much for taking a chance and reading *Sunspots*. Hopefully you enjoyed it. If you did, and want to spread the word, it would be brilliant if you could put a small review on Amazon.

I am currently working on the sequel, which should hopefully be finished and available by late 2016/early 2017. For more info and updates on it, go to:

facebook.com/sunspotsnovel

twitter.com/sunspotsnovel

62662430R00147

Made in the USA
Charleston, SC
20 October 2016